# Rubies and Retribution

## By: Lil Haiti

# Prologue

It was an unusually warm October night on the 300 block of Stillwater Avenue in Stamford, Connecticut, so everyone was out and about shooting the shit and searching for something to get into.

On this night, there was a crisp autumn breeze rustling the leaves of oak and maple trees as Joseph headed to a bodega to get the missing ingredients required for that night's supper. This pleasant draft was a delight to the nose because it carried a savory aroma that caused stomachs to growl.

This scent escaped from Chantal's kitchen as she awaited the return of her husband, Joseph. She was preparing brown rice and peas, red snapper, a tossed salad with a homemade vinaigrette dressing, and her better-than-the-best sweet potato pie.

During his walk, Joseph licked his lips as the tantalizing aromas hypnotized him and everyone on the block.

"Damn! That shit smells good as fuck!" was all he heard from various sources as he walked hand in hand with his miniature twin, Divine. Divine was the four-year-old son he'd parented with Chantal, but father and son shared a stunning resemblance. So much so, friends and family often said he conceived Divine without Chantal.

Arriving at the bodega, Joseph greeted, joked, and exchanged pleasantries with Ahmed, the store's clerk, while Divine rushed to the rear of the establishment to play the arcade games.

Although Divine was out of sight, Joseph didn't worry because he knew exactly where he could be found, if need be. Rather than taking the short trek to the rear of the store, he shouted,

"Hey, Divine!"

"Yes, Daddy," he replied.

"Grab some French vanilla ice cream while you're back there."

"Yay!" he said, as he did his happy dance which consisted of him kicking and jumping around.

Happy to have pleased his only child, Joseph smiled the smile of a proud father, then said, "Ahmed, may I have two scratch-off tickets, some vanilla extract, a pack of Newport cancer sticks, and a tub of French vanilla ice cream, when my boy brings it up to the counter?"

Divine loved arcade games, so he was in heaven playing *Street Fighter*. His favorite player to control was Ryu, so that was who he picked each and every time he played. Ahmed was completely aware of this, so he had a stool made specifically for Divine to accommodate his short stature, so he could handle the joystick.

Looking at his wristwatch for the third time, Joseph noticed how long he'd been on his errand run and knew he'd have to hear his wife's mouth, so he shouted, "Boy, where you at with that ice cream?"

"I'm coming, Daddy," said Divine, as he placed another quarter into the machine after another loss.

"That boy is probably playing the game, Ahmed," said Joseph, as his patience ran thin.

"Probably … that boy of yours is playing the game! There are two things that I know for certain, and they are that a man can't live with or without a woman, and Divine will play that game every time he comes in here," said Ahmed, in response to Joseph's statement.

Finding the humor in the truth of Ahmed's words, Joseph laughed heartily. Then Ahmed joined the laughter as he said, "I love my wife, but she gets upset when I talk about my girlfriend … so you see why I say we can't live with or without them?"

Crying out in hysterical laughter, Joseph said, "You're too much, Ahmed."

Playing coy, Ahmed said, "How am I too much?"

Before Joseph could respond, two masked men entered the bodega, wielding firearms, bringing the laughter to an abrupt halt.

Yelling with a thick Jamaican drawl, one of them demanded, "*No mon no bumba clot move or gunshot a ring! Hey, bwoy, weh di money deh? Cum offa it cuz it nah g' do yu no good if yu mek mi vex!*"

Frozen with fear, Ahmed couldn't comply with the gunmen's request, so they pistol- whipped both him and Joseph to show them that they meant business. Blood gushed from Joseph's head with the force of the waters of Niagara Falls, but he remained calm, in an attempt to give Ahmed strength, but it was too late. Ahmed, on the other hand, was paralyzed with fear as blood oozed out of his nose, so the gunmen ransacked the register and the store's safe.

Remaining completely still, Joseph prayed to the All Merciful to keep Divine put, but his prayers went unheard because he showed up at that very moment with his tiny hands clinging to a tub of Turkey Hill, saying, "Daddy, I got the ice cream."

Hearing Divine's innocent voice, Joseph's heart sank to the pits of his bowels while the gunman turned, ready to open fire with his .45 caliber semi-automatic Sig Sauer. Divine was the most important person in Joseph's life, so he quickly battled his indecisiveness, in regard to fight or flight. He fought.

Tackling the threat to his precious son, Joseph struggled with the masked man while Gunman One shouted, "*Stop play wit di bwoy no, mon!*"

Gasping for breath while using all of his might to free himself from Joseph's clutches, Gunman Two said, "*Di bwoy big an' strong ... Mi cyant box wit him.*"

Joseph was a healthy, working man with a grip tighter than that of a cobra on his assailant's arm to prevent the perpetrator from aiming at his chest. Having a slight advantage over the masked man, he used his other hand to remove the perpetrator's mask, revealing a set of gold teeth encrusted with rubies.

Removing the mask proved to be fatal because Joseph froze when he saw the man's bare face. This moment of hesitation proved to be a grave mistake because it gave the perpetrator time to gather his bearings enough to position his .45 right at Joseph's lungs.

Seizing the moment, he fired once, but two shots rang out. Blocka! Blocka!

The two shots penetrated Joseph's flesh and collapsed his lung. He fell to the ground wheezing, freeing up Gunman Two, who jumped up. He was furious because his partner-in- crime had shot Joseph while he was pinned beneath him, exposing him to the line of fire.

Enraged, Gunman Two's blood simmered, then boiled, so he barked, *"Hey, pussy ole! Yu fiya shot pon mi!"*

Ignoring his cohort's anger, Gunman One said, *"Cum no, mon! Babylon soon cum!"*

Then, he turned to exit the bodega. Unbeknownst to him, those were to be his last words because Gunman Two was really hot from being shot at. He had other plans for his partner in crime, so he gently pressed the warm steel barrel of his .45 to the base of his cohort's skull and said, *"If a pussy ole fiya shot pon mi, a pussy ole must dead!"*

Squeezing the trigger twice, Blocka! Blocka! erupted from the cannon and was the last sound Gunman One heard before his brain was one with the pavement.

In the nearby distance, sirens wailed and could be heard approaching fast, so Gunman Two didn't stick around to see the body drop. He hastily fled the scene, leaving behind a frightened clerk, a distraught four-year-old Divine, and an injured Joseph, who was clinging to life.

Once the coast was clear, Ahmed snapped out of his catatonic state. He was angrier than he'd ever been, so out of sheer frustration, he cursed a storm in his native tongue of Arabic, knocked his empty cash register to the floor, and wept like a baby. He then dialed 911 in hopes of an ambulance and prayed for the life of Joseph. EMT employees were afraid of the neighborhood for various reasons, so they often didn't respond to calls. Two of their own had been shot by the same gunman who had wounded their initial victim because he was on a mission to ensure the death of his first target.

In a state of shock, Divine ran over to where his father was lying in a pool of blood. Scared, confused, and angry, he asked his father to get up. Unable to comply with his son's wishes, Joseph lay practically motionless as life-sustaining fluid exited his torso. His body temperature began to decline, his breathing increased to quick, short shallow breaths, and all of life's beautiful colors began to fade, so he took Divine by the hand and shared his last words with his only son, "Put your pedal to the metal and head for the top spot, Divine! Do you hear me, boy?"

"Yes, Daddy," he replied, as tears flowed from his eyes.

"You can be whatever you want to be in life as long as you try ... whether you decide to be a politician, an actor, a lawyer, a doctor, an architect, or a dope dealer ... you better make sure you're the best one to ever do it because no son of mine will end up a lazy bum! Your dreams can become a reality, no matter how big or small they are, no matter how strange they may seem to the next person, as long as you have the ambition and drive to make them a reality ... Think big, boy! Don't reach for the skies because you'll be selling yourself short. Reach for the next galaxy, so if you happen to fall short, the stars are still within reach ... I love you, boy, and don't you ever forget that. Now get on home and tell your momma I won't be making it for her pie."

"Don't go, Daddy! I need you, Daddy! I love you, Daddy," shouted Divine, as a savage surge of convulsions rocked his body.

As an eerie silence enveloped the bodega, Ahmed comforted Divine as he cradled his dear father in his tiny arms. Words couldn't express the sympathy Ahmed felt for the toddler, so he kept quiet while rubbing the young boy's back until the silence was broken when Joseph said,
"Get on home before that good sweet potato pie gets cold, boy."

"Okay, Daddy."

"One more thing, Divine."

"Anything, Daddy."

"Don't you ever forget the rubies ... the yardy with the rubies."

"What rubies, Daddy?" asked Divine as the last breath and words were shared between father and son.

# Chapter 1

# Twenty-Five Years Later

"No! Don't shoot!" shouted Divine, thrashing around violently on his side of the California king bed he shared with his wife.

"Bae, wake up," said Tessa, gently rousing him from his slumber.

"What? Huh?" asked Divine as he jumped out of his sleep, sweating profusely and panting due to a lack of breath.

"You were having a nightmare. Are you okay?"

"I'm good, love, so go back to sleep."

"You're not good, so stop hiding things from me because I'm your wife … Do you see this?" asked Tessa, as she pointed to the twelve-karat, princess-cut white diamond wedding ring set in eighteen-karat white gold. "Do you know what this ring means, Divine? It means that I'm your other half and that there shouldn't be secrets between us if we are truly one."

"Tessa, there aren't any secrets between us ... I miss my father. That's all. I wish he could've lived long enough to see me grow into a successful business man, even after I stumbled a few times along the way when I was younger."

"Baby, I understand you miss your father, but you're leaving me out in the dark by not telling what it is you see that frightens you so much in your nightmares ..." Switching up to patois, she said, "*Mi fadder back a yard an him big in a thee dream ting, so tell mi so mi cyan chat wit him.*"

"I don't tell you because it's not important. When I feel you need to know, I'll let you know, but until then, don't worry about it."

"Not important!" shouted Tessa, as her beautiful caramel face turned chili pepper red, flushed with anger.

"You wake me up out of my sleep three nights a week, yet you have the audacity to say it's not important."

Vexed, she stood there, burning a hole through his core with her eyes. Her hands were nestled on her hips as one of her breasts peeked from behind her silk negligee. Her nerves were fried from anger, and her foot tapped to the drum of her fury, awaiting an apology or something, but nothing ever came.

Two could play the game, so he stared back at his wife, but with admiration, rather than malice. Her beauty was extraordinary. It was even evident to the visually impaired. Although tempers flared, she looked so tasty because her bright red face matched the ruby earrings her father had given her when she was a teenager. She was simply delectable, but rather than letting her beauty cloud his judgment, he shouted, "Sleep … that's what this is about, Tessa? Your precious sleep? Fine … you can have as much sleep as a man in a coffin because I'll be sleeping in the guest room from now on."

He knew his outburst was uncalled for, but he couldn't back down, so he grabbed his favorite comforter, which was made by Gucci, then headed for the east wing of his nine-thousand square foot mansion.

"Don't act like that because I'm only concerned for my husband ... am I wrong for that?"

Attempting to defuse the bomb that could ruin their marriage proved to be fruitless because her words fell on deaf ears since Divine was already halfway across the central foyer in pursuit of some solitude in the east wing.

\*\*\*

The night was young, and Divine was restless, so it would be senseless to try to fall back asleep because sleep would elude him. Unfortunately, bad dreams came often, creating a routine, so he kept to tradition by grabbing an ice-cold

Guinness from the fridge, then headed to his rather expensive recording studio designed by Francis Manzella.

Seated behind his mix board, he exhaled his frustrations, then powered up his studio. His workstation was designed so all his gear was within arm's reach, and it was on wheeled racks that could be pulled to or pushed away when need be.

Divine was a successful record label owner with his partners, an engineer, a programmer, a songwriter and a producer, so his home studio was equipped with forty-eight motorized faders on his D-command recording console. He'd had his console set up in a sweet spot that was eight feet from his main mixing monitors, so everything was crystal clear when it came time for a pristine recording and mix down.

Wrapping around from the left-hand side were all his processors, compressors, pre-amps and samplers. Smack dab in the middle was an Apple iMac desktop computer, boasting 32-gigabytes of ram to ensure speed when multi-tracking large projects. To his right were his keyboards, drum machines, and guitars.

His studio was his safe haven. It brought him peace of mind. Plus, it churned out three number one Billboard chart toppers every week. His nightmares were his inspiration, so he'd go into the studio and create party, upbeat, and high energy music that was reminiscent of the famous producer Swizz Beats.

One would think he would make dark, gloomy tracks after these nightmares, but they always had the opposite effect. They gave him the motivation to make music that brought people's moods up rather than down.

During these sessions in what he called "nightmare studios," he went hard because his father had told him that he needed to have ambition and drive to be successful in life. He banged on the pads of his Akai MPC 2000XL sampler and the keys to his Yamaha Motif XS and Roland

Fantom keyboards, composing tracks into the wee hours of the morning. He would rock nonstop, shaking the house with heavy bass lines until his eyes were too heavy to keep open. Once fatigue set in and he felt he had a few bangas, he would store and save them to his CPU's internal hard drive. As a safety measure, he also stored his files in an external 1 terabyte Western Digital hard drive, just in case his computer crashed.

Once everything was shut down and he was satisfied with the session, he would kick his feet up onto his coffee table, close his eyes, and say, "Those hits are for you, Dad."

Then, he'd fall asleep.

***

"Good morning, Daddy!"

The greeting echoed through the immaculate kitchen that was designed by Scott Pierce's custom cabinets as Divine's princesses gathered around the solid hardwood oak dining room table.

"Where are your manners, girls? I say that because I know your father isn't the only person you see in here?" asked Tessa.

"Good morning, Mommy," said the girls.

"That's more like it," she replied, happy to be greeted by her offspring.

Trinity was the eldest of the three. Mentally, she was twenty-one years old. She was extremely bright and witty, and she carried herself with a demeanor that was so calm and laidback that most people assumed she was older than her seven years.

Divinity was their second oldest child, who was five years old. She was fun-loving and adorable with a stunning resemblance to both Tessa and Chantal, Divine's mother. Her imagination was out of this world. It was so colorful that it belittled those of the children's show *Muppet Babies*.

Serenity was the baby at four, but she had earned herself the nickname B-G because that was exactly what she was — a baby gangsta. She was tiny in stature but rowdy and aggressive, similar to Scrappy Doo on *Scooby Doo*. This aggression was a trait inherited from Divine, but it was rarely seen in him at this stage of his life.

"What's for breakfast, Mommy?" asked Trinity, as she thumbed through a *Jet* magazine.

"We're having French toast, scrambled eggs, and Canadian bacon or sausage, with your choice of orange, apple, or grapefruit juice."

"That's what I'm talking about, Mommy," said Trinity.

"Aww, man," was Divinity's reply because cereal was her favorite food.

She loved cereal so much that Divine would often joke that, if he'd left her home alone for a month with a surplus of milk and Captain Crunch, she wouldn't notice everyone was gone due to her overactive imagination.

"Mommy, may I have some cereal?"

"No, you may not have cereal because I slaved over this stove to give you a hot, balanced, and tasty breakfast."

"Okay, Mommy."

"Thank you for understanding, Divinity, and for that reason, you may have cereal for lunch today and breakfast tomorrow."

"Yay! Thank you, Mommy."

"You're welcome, baby," replied Tessa, mussing Divinity's hair.

"Ma, all I want is sausage," said B-G.

"Sausage alone won't fill you up, honey."

"Yes, it will, if you fill up the plate."

Hearing his ladies go back and forth, Divine laughed because B-G was one hundred percent right. His baby gangsta had her own unique way of looking at things that almost always made sense and turned out right.

With everyone seated, Tessa served breakfast and said grace, and they all dug into their meals. The food was delicious, so they ate quietly for a minute before Tessa broke the silence saying, "B-G, since you're next to your father, could you ask him to pass me the maple syrup?"

"He heard you, Ma," she replied, in between bites of sausage.

"I'm tired of your slick mouth, little girl! You're going on punishment as soon as you wash these dishes."

"No, I'm not because I didn't do nothing wrong … Tell her, Daddy."

"Enough! You're not on punishment, B-G, and here's your maple syrup, Tessa. You can't get mad at her because you're upset with me … Now let's not ruin this good breakfast. We still need to get the girls packed and ready to see your father in Ocho Rios."

Hearing this, Trinity cheered, "Yay! Grandpa Ricardo!"

And the other two cheered.

"I guess it's safe to say you're not coming, Divine," said Tessa, unable to hide her feelings of disappointment.

"Bae, you know I'd love to go, but I have a lot on my plate with this label and production company."

"I'm starting to think you're trying to avoid meeting my father … is that the case?"

"No, Tessa … I promise I'll go with you next year, okay?"

"I'm holding you to that, Divine."

"A'ight," said Divine, but if he knew that Jamaica would be the answer to all his problems, he'd have flown there years ago.

The beautiful but dangerous island was all it would take to find the answers he'd been seeking for the last twenty-five years, but was he prepared to deal with the truth?

# Chapter 2

# Eleven Years Ago

Divine and his team, the Haitian Mob, were hood, the epitome of a product of their environment. They were hybrids, a cross between hustlers and gangstas. A fine line separated the two from one another, but true street niggas knew the difference.

At the tender age of eighteen, Divine had already seen, done, and been through more than a person three times his age. And for this reason, he carried himself with an air of confidence that demanded respect.

He and his air-tight team of Haitians ran through the middle-class city among different sects of wolves with only a few concerns. One was being able to obtain the riches that would elevate them to the next tax bracket. The second was to bring death to anyone who attempted to take the silver spoon they so desperately desired.

Stamford, Connecticut was a gold mine! The city itself generated tons of money due to all the big businesses it was home to. Sweetening the pot was the fact that it was located snuggly between two of Connecticut's wealthiest towns — Greenwich was to the south, and conveniently to the north was Darien — which awarded the hustlers in Stamford big pay days from corporate executives, lawyers, doctors, judges, athletes, and Wall Street traders.

Ever the opportunists, Divine, Playboy, T-Gunz, K-Blizz, Robbery Rob, Young Swiss, and Blacky Black realized that the possibilities to explode were endless, so they did their groundwork and made their ascent to the top.

Lil Haiti

They were a force to be reckoned with but were solely about their money. They were a clique that didn't really care or thrive off beef like other crews, but if a mothafucka and his squad got out of line, machetes got sharpened, guns went off, candles got lit, and they embraced the gangsta shit with open arms.

Whether the members of the Haitian Mob were born back home or in the states, they had a spirit of protection or a guardian angel guiding them, heightening their instincts, so the life of crime came easy.

They eluded arrest after arrest, so the streets began to talk. Speculation of protection from voodoo came from the mouths of admirers, and slanderous accusations of cooperating with the authorities came from haters, but it didn't matter to the Mob because they knew what it was. They alone knew their protection was kept safely in their possession in the form of Haitian flags blessed by a voodoo priestess, so what was said about them wasn't any of their concerns.

They had the brains, brawn, and protection to green light all their illegal endeavors for the duration of their lives as long as they followed the rules, but weren't rules made to be broken?

***

Lounging at Leone Park, better known as Jamaica Park, on a beautiful day, Playboy and Blacky Black took a quick break to burn it down before they went back to their grind. Seated on a park bench as the yard men played cricket and smoked and steamed fish, the fellas relaxed and ducked the ever-present police prescence on Stillwater. Ladies were everywhere, living by the mantra: "If you got it, flaunt it," so the Mob's eyes followed, and their hearts admired the voluptuous women scantily clad in revealing fishnet outfits, but they did not break their conversation to chase skirts.

In his native tongue of Creole, Playboy said, "What up, my nigga?"

"*Sak passé zozo'm?*"

"*Ou gintan konin,*" responded Blacky Black, before he translated, saying, "I said you already know." Black knew Playboy understood, but there was a joke among the team that Playboy's Creole was garbage, so they were constantly picking at him.

Responding in Creole, Playboy said, "Fuck you."

"*Get momma' ou*" translated to "Fuck you."

Then he switched back to English, saying, "Stop tryna play me, nigga. I know what the fuck you said."

After sharing a lighthearted laugh and their smoke, Playboy flicked the roach into a puddle of spilled beer, and the two men went back to getting money. They hustled on Stamford's west side where there was a frenzy for the cream like sharks in a tank full of bloody seals. They ran in and out of the three housing complexes — Connecticut Avenue (Conn Ave), Merrell Avenue, and Fairfield Avenue (F.F.I) — all for the mighty dollar. They did dirt on Spruce Street, Stephen Street, and Rose Park. Any street on the west that had the potential to be opened up was where they were found. They each did their own thing, but profits were split down the middle, generating a bigger slice of the pie for each member.

Divine moved both soft and hard, Playboy moved ecstasy, Robbery Rob's name was self-explanatory, and Young Swiss distributed pounds of haze. T-Gunz was a gunrunner who'd disappear for weeks at a time, then reemerge from his absence with brand new Macs, Techs, AKs, and every hand canon known to man. Blacky Black moved heroin, and K-Blizz was a ladies' man who, for some strange reason, only attracted women with financial stability that would spoil the whole team, just to keep him happy. He'd remove the women from his roster once their (or in some cases their husbands') accounts were depleted.

\*\*\*

It was Friday and the block party at Friendship Park was poppin'. Friendship was a nine-story high rise, but don't get fooled by the name because there wasn't a damn thing soft, sweet, or friendly about its residents.

On this night, women were out in packs, searching for a good time, while fellas were out on the prowl, in hopes of one-night stands. DJ Vance spun the latest tracks by the hottest rap, R&B, and pop artists. Hoop ballers ran full court under the street lights while hood ballas made substantial wagers on their favorite teams. Drunk uncles manned the grills, talking shit, all while flirting with girls young enough to be their daughters.

The streets were buzzing about the event, so the Mob, minus Playboy, T-Gunz, and Young Swiss broke the rules by abandoning the block on its biggest payday to make an appearance.

When they arrived at the gathering, the Mob acknowledged and spread love to those they knew and kept a close eye on the small few they didn't. They mingled, burned it down, and went to war with the customary gallon of Hennessy they kept in tow. Spectators watched as the hood celebrities made their presence felt. Ladies sauntered around in a variety of ensembles. Those of them in their teens and early twenties wore skin-tight booty shorts, Jordan sneakers, and belly shirts to show off navel rings. The more mature and established women wore fitted dresses to accent their curves. Their stilettos and clutches were fitting complements.

Throughout all the fun and games, everyone smiled and enjoyed the night because there hadn't been any fights, stabbings, or shootings. What put the icing on the cake and made things better for the Mob was that four big booty freaks from a housing complex across town called Southfield Village or South Kill approached them with intentions of doing what adults do.

Hours passed and the Mob had smoked and drank with the community while making small talk with their victims for the night — Tasha, Rhonda, Tameka, and Angel. Their conversations were laced with sexual innuendo, so they made a hasty retreat to the Stamford Suites to do the damn thing.

Once situated in their luxury suite, equipped with a master bedroom, kitchen, a living room, and a dining room, Rob quickly stripped to his boxer shorts and socks, provoking Rhonda to say, "Unh-unh ... this nigga buggin'."

"How I'm buggin'?" asked Rob, incredulously.

"Can't we just chill?" she asked, feeling a bit self-conscious when she noticed her girls were following Rob's lead by removing their clothing.

"We ain't come here to chill and watch *SportsCenter* … we here to fuck … if you wanna chill, take ya ass back to Friendship," said Rob, smacking Tameka's ass as she passed by.

"Relax, girl," said Tasha, because she was dying to fuck Blacky Black. "You wit' good niggas, so let's have a good time."

"For real," said Divine, in between licks of Angel's perky nipples.

"I hear y'all, but y'all loose … y'all getting it in like ain't nobody else in the room," said Rhonda, observing her first orgy.

"Ain't nobody in the room but us," said Divine. "Ain't nothing but good dick, pussy, and, hopefully, good head in this mothafucka, so what you wanna do? 'Cause niggas tryna switch … I could tell you got that grease … and we all want some."

"Hopefully?" asked Angel. "This head the truth," she said, before taking him into her mouth.

Having been convinced, along with being witness to the sights and sounds of passion, Rhonda finally accepted K-Blizz's sexual advancements and joined the cacophony of lust. The room was engulfed with animalistic lust where hips gyrated, breasts were squeezed, asses were smacked, and lips slurped pre-cum out of excited penises. Cocks were thrust deep into tight wombs repeatedly, causing legs to tremble from climax. Positions and partners were switched to four women on the edges of the bed, faces down with their asses up, two per side, facing one another, in such close proximity their lips grazed in an introduction to lesbianism. The guys stood tall from behind, stroking to their own rhythms. Heavy penetration caused the girls to wail loud enough for the neighboring rooms to suspect the occupants were auditioning for an opera. The guys dived deep and exchanged hi-fives in delight as they swam in the new, unchartered pussies.

The fuck session was intense, and it went on for hours until every person, but Rhonda, passed out. This was the first time her poor coochie had experienced such an energetic escapade, so her body ached, and her vagina was swollen like a balloon. She and her girls had taken four cocks each, varying in length and girth, but she was out of commission. To remedy the situation, she headed for the tub to soak in scalding water. As she soaked, the steaming water soothed her throbbing body, so she replayed what would make a seasoned porn star blush in her mind's eye. Recalling what transpired between her and the Mob, she smiled and said, "That was fun," but vowed to never do it again, then exited the tub. After drying her lean, taut body, she wrapped herself in a warm, plush towel, then headed back to the master bedroom where condoms were strewn everywhere. Disgusted, she began to discard the used latex until she spotted the famous Haitian flags hanging from the rear right pockets of the Mob's jeans. Having a need for a souvenir to remember the day she was sexually liberated, she broke the rules by touching and stealing these prized possessions. Unaware of the repercussions of her actions, she climbed back into the bed, snuggled up to K-Blizz and joined the tangled mess of bodies.

***

While seated at the round table, sipping five-star Barbancourt Haitian rum, playing 32, a game of poker, the Mob bickered about the loss of their Haitian flags.

"I think them shits fell out at Friendship," said K-Blizz, grimacing from the burn caused by the rum flowing through his chest.

"Me, too," said Rob, raising another fifty dollars in the hand of poker.

Confident on his full house, Black raised another hundred dollars without a care in the world for his boys' concerns over the missing flags.

"Nah ... they ain't at Friendship 'cause I had my joint at the telly," said Divine.

"You sure?" asked Rob, while calling Black's bet.

"Hell, yeah ... I think them bitches snatched them," said Divine, after taking a healthy swig of rum.

"Why the fuck would they do some shit like that when they coulda took bread instead?" asked K-Blizz.

"'Cause niggas is trophy dick to them bitches," replied Black. "All eyes was on them cuz they was wit us ... they ain't gonna steal cuz they know better and will do anything to be around niggas ... they proved that wit the session we had."

"I hear that, but what if them bitches did take em?" asked Divine. "We gonna be hit 'cause the voodoo lady said chicks can't touch 'em."

"Don't start trippin', nigga," said Rob. "They fell out at the Exit 6 gas station when niggas was getting condoms and shit."

"The fuck you mean 'don't trip'? If them bitches touched shit, all types of foul shit gonna happen to niggas," said K-Blizz.

"Chill the fuck out 'cause y'all fuckin' up my high," said Rob. "I'mma go see her soon and get some new joints."

Rob was the elder of the crew, so for the moment, his words subdued the guys enough to relax and begin formulating a strategy to exit the game. They all were high school graduates or GED recipients, so the opportunities were endless, but neither of them knew what they could do to afford the luxurious lifestyle they'd grown accustomed to.

Unable to figure out a path, they remained undecided for weeks and that proved to be too long because Blacky Black caught a body in the Ps over his baby's mother.

On a regular Tuesday night, Blacky Black decided to spend some time with his son's mother to stop her nagging, but all went to hell when they were taking a walk through Merrell Avenue. They were hand in hand when some fool ran up, smacking the taste out of her mouth. He claimed she burned him with chlamydia, but Black didn't take heed to the allegation of her infidelity and reacted off impulse, reaching for his Glock-19, equipped with an extended thirty shot magazine. Taught to never pull out without intentions of use, Black dumped seven shots into the kid's face.

There was a crowd of thirty gathered at the time of the incident, and the majority of them were women who would have normally kept quiet, but with homicide detectives threatening to have their children placed in the custody of the Department of Children and Family Services for interfering with an investigation, they quickly cooperated.

The spiritual protection that usually loomed over Black, keeping him out of handcuffs, was no longer by his side, so he found himself in an unfamiliar position, which was posting bail. Once he stepped out of the precinct, he thought of the fun times that had led to the moment, gathered $200,000, and went on the run, but he was apprehended in the Midwest, in Portland, Oregon, for a completely different charge. He was arrested and arraigned for the charges of assault in the first degree, possession of a deadly weapon, and resisting arrest for pistol whipping a wannabe tough guy who had bumped him at a Sonic's fast food chain. Those petty charges were run concurrently to the thirty-five-year sentence imposed on him after being extradited to Connecticut.

***

The bad news about Black rocked the Mob, but it wasn't quite over because bad news always came in threes. The second installment of ill fate came shortly after Black's when news came of Robbery-Rob and K-Blizz running up in a Columbian kingpin's place with their guns blazing.

Rob had gathered intel from an undisclosed source, stating the kingpin had twenty million (and growing) in cash, plus two hundred kilos of grade-A cocaine that had never been looked at, so he paired with Blizz to make a move on the unsuspecting drug lord.

After surveilling the drug czar's mini-mansion for weeks, Rob and Blizz opted against taking it by storm because the estate was flooded with security and equipped with military grade weaponry.

Jaime was a native of Bogotá, Columbia. He was a no-nonsense type of guy with a reputation for only dealing with the upper echelon of the underworld. He was a guy who'd shun and scoff at two or three kilo purchasers because he had access to an entire cocaine plantation. He was a shrewd businessman who'd only succumb to a purchaser of five kilos, if his gut instinct held that person in high regard.

After countless hours of fruitless surveillance seated in Rob's Lexus GS 400, the guys quickly concluded that someone was needed on the inside to arrange a meeting that would grant them access to what Jaime had to offer. Blizz was fed up with the waiting game, so he said, "We could use Cashmere to get good wit' this guala ... she is the baddest bitch this side of the galaxy, so we gonna be good."

"That bitch tough ... don't know how ya ugly ass bagged that ... she speak that tricky shit, too, so we good."

"Yeah, she speak that shit fluent ... all we gotta do is have them meet, and she'll do the rest."

"Since niggas been layin' on 'em, you peeped how he hit the Dominican massage parlor on Tuesdays and Thursdays, so all we gotta do is get her plugged in at the spot. From there, we got his ass ... can ya bitch give a massage?"

"I don't know 'bout all that ... but I do know she could suck a mean dick," said Blizz, chuckling.

The statement tickled their funny bones, so they laughed and chopped it up for a while, then put their plan in motion.

That following Monday, Cashmere, resembling a slice of heaven, strutted into the massage parlor Jaime frequented, displaying her assets, which was a gorgeous face accompanied by the measurements of 36D, 22, 44. For a better depiction of this character, picture a five-foot, seven-inch hourglass.

The décor of Tropical Massage was akin to Cashmere because it to was breathtakingly beautiful. The establishment exuded tranquility with white furniture, scented candles, and framed pictures of the world's most alluring beaches. Freshly spruced flowers illuminated the waiting room with bright hues of pink, yellow, blue, and magenta. Stress melted upon entering the premises, so Cashmere understood why one would frequent the relaxation center.

After ringing a countertop bell for assistance, Cashmere waited patiently in a revealing, strapless formfitting sundress. Her presence could not be ignored, so the manager, startled by her beauty, stumbled over his words, skipped the entire application process, and hired her on the spot, without even caring about her ability to give a massage. In his eyes, she was the epitome of perfection, so the only qualification she was required to have was the one she was born with — the art of seduction.

"Can you start today?" he asked, eager to keep her flawless beauty in his presence.

"Oh, no ... I'm sorry," she said, knowing the sway of her hips had him hypnotized. "I have a few errands to attend to, so tomorrow will be better, if that's okay with you?"

"Okay, no problem. Tomorrow, it is," he said, unable to mask his disappointment.

Beaming with a radiant smile, she said, "Thank you for the opportunity."

"No, thank you. The pleasure is all mine," said the manager, as he toyed with images of bending her over one of his massage tables.

Cashmere was witty and completely aware of the sexual innuendo underlying his words, so she took full advantage of his lustful thoughts, asking, "May I suggest a bit of advice, sir?"

"Yes, sure, as long as it brings in more money, Cashmere."

"I think you'd earn more revenue if you allowed your girls the freedom to have themes, because it would turn the massage experience into a fantasy. What do you think, sir? I only mention this because I have a naughty police uniform I've been dying to wear," said Cashmere, with a devilish grin.

"Brains, beauty, and a world of booty ... I like it! Wear whatever and as little as you'd like, and I'll post a memo for the girls by noon."

"Thank you, sir."

"No, thank you. And call me Sammy."

"Okay. I'll see you in the morning, Sammy."

\*\*\*

"Today is a good day" was the silent thought shared between Divine and Playboy as they sat on a park bench on Merrell Avenue behind Building 52. Divine was also contemplating escaping the drug game because of what had happened to Blacky Black and because the success rate for retiring from the game was lower than low.

After stewing in their own thoughts, they exited the park, bought ice cream cones for the kids from Mista Softee and walked through the housing projects, where they were acknowledged with comments such as, "What's poppin', homie?" from the fellas and, "Damn, girl ... who them niggas?" from women visiting friends and family. They were the Haitian Mob, celebrities in their own right, loved by the ladies and hated by the niggas who weren't running with their clique, yet they were respected by all.

Earlier in the day, at around one, before sitting in the park, strategizing, Divine stepped on the block with twenty dollars in his pocket, but it was now four in the afternoon, and he had already accumulated $5,000, distributing quarters, halves, and whole ounces of hard to the youngens on the come-up. Playboy, on the other hand, had had a slow start but was gaining ground by earning $3,500 moving the party drug ecstasy to the rollers.

Money was coming in; it was a beautiful day, and so far, no shots had rung out, causing Divine to say, "There's only one thing missing to complete the day."

Playboy knew Divine as well as he knew himself, so in unison, they said, "New pussy!"

The day was young, so there was enough time to slide off to get their dicks out of the desert, then come back to sting the block for the late-night rush, but before they departed, Divine said, "Damn! Shorty tough. Who that?"

The magnificent specimen of a woman that caught his full attention was a brown-skinned bombshell. She stood at five feet, seven inches tall and weighed in at a hundred-sixty pounds. There was nothing fat or sloppy about her because her one hundred-sixty was all in her hips, thighs, and booty. She wore wavy, shoulder-length hair accented with brown streaks to compliment her mocha complexion. Adding icing to her cake was a tiny waist that placed emphasis on her large derrière and double-D breasts. She was tough, and her walk was mean! So mean, it had Divine's jaw hanging to the pavement. Disgusted at witnessing Divine out of character, Playboy slapped him behind the head and said, "Pick ya mouth up wit ya ugly ass ... you a Mob nigga that got hoes, so act right."

Laughing at Playboy's remark, Divine thought of a slick comment, but before he could formulate the words, Playboy said, "Her name is Infinity, and she's the new thang that moved in Building 42 on the fifth floor. I caught her comin' from Julio's bodega lookin' sweet as a pineapple, so I spit the gift, she gave my pretty ass rhythm, and now it's poppin for the night ... you know what the best part is?"

"Nah, what's good?"

"She told me to bring a friend ... I got you ... I'm always lookin' out for ya big-ass head ... yo ... I forgot to put you on wit' something."

"What you forgot?"

"Oh, yeah ... I saw a breakin' news bulletin tellin' why white people had our ancestors pickin' cotton."

"You bluffin' ... they ain't show no shit like that."

"Listen, nigga ... they said the reason was to make sure they had enough material to make a fitted for ya big-ass head."

Laughing, Divine said, "Fuck you, nigga. I'm goin' to the liquor store, so I'll scream at you later."

"Make sure you pick up ya jack when I hit you ... be easy out here 'cause I'm 'bout to get that fire from

Linden and Powell ... I ain't smoke all day! My lungs feel clean as fuck, so I gotta put it in the air."

"Ya shorty girl better be tough 'cause I ain't fuckin' wit no mud duck ... I want a pretty ass peacock, swan, or flamingo. You put ya dick in dimes and negative fours, and I ain't around for that."

"You good, B ... trust me," said Playboy, sucking his teeth with a sly smile plastered all over his face.

"Trust you?" exclaimed Divine incredulously. "Last time I got up wit' a bitch you provided, the bitch was bigger than that nigga in *The Green Mile*."

"You stupid," said Playboy, in between fits of laughter.

"Nigga, am I lyin'?"

"You got me there ... you a real nigga for takin' that one for the team."

"You lucky I love you 'cause I didn't know what to think when she was grillin me wit' what she thought was a seductive look. I didn't know if she was feelin' me or wanted a head up … I almost pulled the strap out on her big ass."

"Nigga, you stupid," said Playboy, as hysterical laughter erupted from the pits of his belly.

"I woulda clapped that big bitch … you think it's a game? She was six two and two o' five, so I wasn't 'bout to box wit' her."

"You wasn't sayin' that when you was splashin' in the pussy, though."

"Hell no … she had good guts and was pretty … her problem was she big as hell … fuckin' Amazon."

"That pussy was good like that? I gotta get me some."

"Hell yeah! I slid off on y'all niggas many nights to go stab that … but enough of that … what her girl look like?"

"I don't know, but if she got a dome like you y'all gonna look like two hot air balloons."

Going their separate ways, Divine played PlayStation, ate, and relaxed for a while. After recouping his energy from a quick nap, he washed up and shook off the anxiety aimed at the night's rendezvous. Deciding against wearing Prada, Gucci, Fendi or Louis, he opted for a comfortable Polo sweatsuit, a Yankee fitted, a white T-shirt, white Harlems (Uptowns), big jewelry, and a touch of his favorite cologne, Envy by Gucci.

Stepping back on the scene, looking, feeling, and smelling like money, Divine parked his Cadillac CTS behind Building 74 in an alley behind Merrell Avenue. His ride was laced, equipped with an Alpine deck, J-L Audio amplifiers pushing J-L Audio subs, mids, and tweeters. An Optimus battery was located in the trunk to generate extra power and relieve pressure from the battery and alternator. Seven-inch screens were mounted in the headrests accompanied by a monstrous 20-inch Panasonic to provide a platform to view the latest DVDs. The exterior was equally plush, fitted with an Asanti grill and rim package.

While making his way through the housing complex in search of Playboy, Divine spotted a dice game that could occupy his time, so he tried his luck to bide time until the jumpoff jumped off. Rolling head crack after head crack, he stung Trife Trigga, Bad News, and Yayo for six stacks in cee-lo, then linked up with Playboy to get the night started.

Seated on cement benches with Playboy at his side, Divine sipped Hennessy restlessly because his phone was going crazy with booty calls he was turning down in pursuit of new pussy. Divine was very impatient by nature, and he was a few minutes away from losing his cool, but he reasoned with himself, thinking, Ain't nothing in this world better than pussy but new pussy.

"Fix ya face 'cause you actin' like shit ain't 'bout to pop off … they'll be here in a minute," said Playboy, as he flicked the ash from his blunt.

"They better 'cause I turned down a whole city's worth of guaranteed pussy for some maybe pussy."

Divine was hot and prepared to talk more shit until he spotted Infinity's hourglass frame in his peripheral, strutting through the alley, coming from Stillwater, toward them.

Although Divine was full-blooded Haitian, he spoke with Jamaican patois, saying, "Di gyal pretty … when mi say pretty … mi mean like money!"

Infinity sashayed toward them with her hips swaying in slow motion, hypnotizing both men and women alike with her walk. The cool breeze caused her nipples to be fully erect as her double-D cups slightly bounced with every step. She was bad, so bad that a few guys who were out with their girls were slapped because they couldn't help but look when she passed by.

"I don't see her girl, nigga … if all my booty calls got up wit' their boyfriends or other niggas, I'm fuckin' you up … I'm out."

"Here she come right now … chill, nigga."

When she reached the guys, she greeted them both with an infectious smile, warm hug, and kiss on the cheek, but Divine met her coldly. "Where's ya girl?"

"That bitch frontin', but I got an idea to guarantee we all have a good time."

"What you got in mind?" asked Playboy.

"Can't a girl have secrets? Be easy 'cause I got this, Playboy."

Impatience, along with a zero-tolerance policy for people's bullshit, caused Divine to say,

"I ain't got time for this shit … I'm out."

Infinity wasn't feeling Divine's attitude and refused to let him ruin her night, so she grabbed him by the arm, pulled him in close with sad puppy eyes, and said, "I don't want you to leave, daddy."

Sex oozed from her every syllable, causing Divine to get rock hard with thoughts of slaying her big, fat booty. After having his interest peaked, he decided to stick around for a while to have a shot at turning his thoughts into reality.

The trio didn't have any intentions of sitting in the hood and doing nothing, so they followed Infinity's lead and took Playboy's Lincoln LS to an upscale gentlemen's club named Extreme Satisfaction.

She had her night mapped out and wasn't going to let anyone intervene, so she kept a close eye on Divine. First, she figured she'd get the guys tipsy on Remy XO. Then, she'd get their blood flowing southbound by having them around a heap of pussy. From there, if her plan went accordingly, she'd be able to get home and split fourteen or more inches between them.

Arriving at Satisfaction, the trio spotted beautiful women everywhere. They were on stage gyrating, behind the bar serving drinks, and situated at booths enjoying lap dances. Music blasted from mammoth speakers, shaking the establishment loose from its foundation. Everyone in attendance in the place to be had a ball and partied hard like they didn't have any cares in the world. The gang sipped top-shelf liquor, blew fire green, made it rain for the ladies shaking what their mothers blessed them with, groped exotic dancers during lap dances, and danced to the beat on the dance floor. Strobe lights flashed as sexy bodies melded into one another. The guys placed Infinity in a sandwich where she threw her big ole booty on Divine. Face to face with Playboy, she hungrily nibbled his bottom lip. This went on for a few hours or so with them switching positions back and forth until body temperatures raised, leaving them hot and bothered.

The flirting, caressing, and dancing was too much of a tease for Divine, so he said, "We out," then paid the tab.

Playboy wasn't a heavy drinker, so he was very inebriated, in no condition to drive, but Divine was a professional drunk driver, so he handled the LS through traffic with ease.

Weaving around pedestrians, he headed straight to the Stamford Suites where he had reserved a room earlier in the day. Once there, they took a three-way shower where Divine lathered Infinity's juicy breasts from his position behind her while she thoroughly cleansed Playboy's cock. She then turned to face Divine and proceeded to scrub him from head to toe all while admiring the tattoos of his mother's name on his forearm and the words THINK BIG on his back. Her swollen clitoris throbbed as the scar on his abdomen appeared from beneath soap suds and she became curious about its origin. Intensifying her arousal was Playboy, who was gently kissing, licking, and sucking her clit from behind. Her body shuddered from anticipation as Divine spread her ass cheeks to finger her booty slowly. Playboy continued to lick gracefully until he found out how many licks it took to get to the center of her Tootsie Pop.

Once out of the shower, Infinity dried them both off, applied lotion to their bodies, and directed them to the bed, where they fed one another fruit from an Edible Arrangements basket. She sucked on their fingers as they fed her grapes, chocolate-covered strawberries, and honey dew and drove them insane with anticipation about how good her mouth would feel on their blood-filled organs.

Divine was a take charge kind of guy, so he laid her down on her stomach to deliver a full-body baby oil rubdown. He had recently purchased a new Johnson & Johnson lubricant that warmed when applied, so this was the opportunity to test it out before introducing it to his regular stable of women. He massaged her shoulders all while planting tender kisses to the nape of her neck. He took to kneading her upper and lower back as if it was dough, caressed and squeezed her fleshy booty, and rubbed her thick, tasty thighs. All the while, Playboy sucked her toes.

In ecstasy, she gasped, then said, "Y'all niggas dangerous together! Y'all tryna have a bitch fucked up, but if it feels this good to be dizzy on the dick, don't stop. Get it, get it."

Feeling like a queen, she floated on cloud nine because she had two hard-body niggas having their way with her. She was acting out a fantasy that many women had, but were too afraid to experience. They were too afraid to release their inner freaks for fear of having their business broadcasted in the street. The only thing she felt was missing were two servants ... one with a big peacock feather to fan her and another feeding her grapes while her lovers manhandled her.

Divine, then, lay on his back, seating her above his face, so he could lick and lick until he tasted her creamy milkshake. The tongue job she was receiving was so wicked that it caused her to grind her wet pussy into his face as he squeezed and caressed her ample bosom. He then pulled her forward, bending her at the waist, positioning her remarkable booty in the air, so Playboy could eat her ass while he licked the kitten. Spreading her cheeks so he could get the job done properly, Playboy licked, kissed, sucked, and blew cool air on her asshole which, in turn, caused her to coo with delight.

"Don't stop, Playboy! Eat this ass! Ooh … suck that pussy, Divine," she said, while reaching back to hold her cheeks apart and trembling from her climax. "I can't take no more … one of y'all better put some dick in this wet-wet 'cause I need penetration … deep penetration," she said, jumping off Divine's face to position herself at the edge of the bed with her face down and ass up, prepared for some serious back shots.

Lying beneath her, loving the heat from her D-cups as they rested on his thighs, Playboy moaned as she devoured his manhood greedily. She licked him like a lollipop, deep throating him to the best of her ability, pausing only to lick his shaft and suckle his testicles.

Divine watched her put in work on his boy for a second, then entered her love muscle slowly. He went to the depths of her ocean, exploring every inch of her underwater cavern. He stroked, grinded, and beat the pussy up while fingering her ass. She sucked Playboy tighter and faster as she neared her climax. As his toes curled, he squeezed her breasts as he neared his own. Divine was on a mission to please and to be pleased, so he stroked harder, deeper, and faster because he was in line to explode, too.

After another thirty minutes of intense sex, they came in unison. Infinity swallowed Playboy's load as she released hers onto Divine's eight inches, leaving her thick cream on his condom. Divine was to come next, so he pulled out, removed the latex and came on her fatty.

The night was young, and libidos were high, so they cleaned up and started round two. Anxious to send her over the edge with a big-O, Playboy produced some K-Y Jelly, in order to lubricate her booty in preparation for anal intercourse. While he did this, she valiantly attempted to suck the soul out of Divine through his shaft.

"Ooh ... you nasty, Playboy," she said, wiggling her big ole booty as he fingered her ass to loosen her enough to take his heavy cock in her back door.

She had fun with the dick as she sucked, licked, and tried her best to deep throat him. She suckled his balls and kissed the helmet while holding his member in her hand, saying, "I love this dick."

Having finally lubed her enough to take his tool in the rear comfortably, Playboy said,

"Captain, I'm goin' in."

"Do ya duty and serve ya country proudly, soldier," she said, as she reached behind to spread her cheeks to allow him room for maximum penetration.

Playboy stroked and stroked until Infinity's eyes rolled into the back of her head. It was poppin' in the suite, so after forty-five minutes of heavy panting and grunting, they came in unison once more. Playboy couldn't take the torment of watching her big booty bounce every which way any longer because the jiggle of a big ass was a black man's kryptonite. The waves to her booty were too much to bear, so he came in her ass as she came all over him, trembling uncontrollably and screaming, "Fuck! You good dick bastards … I hate y'all."

In response to her comment, Playboy said, "I love you, too, you nasty bitch."

Divine came hard, and she swallowed the bulk of his protein shake. What she didn't swallow, she rubbed onto her lips and face while stroking his tool to release every drop.

After the drinking, the smoking, and the intense session, Playboy fell fast asleep to her left with his head on a breast. She lay snuggly between them, dizzy off dick, while Divine was to her right with his head on her other breast, thinking things were going too well, so something wasn't right. She, on the other hand, was elated with a smile as wide as the Cheshire cat from *Alice in Wonderland*. Exhausted from a sexual royal rumble, she rested with a penis in each hand and drifted off to sleep with the thought, Today was a good day.

***

Entering Tropical Massage, Cashmere said, "Hi," and introduced herself in her native tongue of Spanish.

"*Buenos dias*, Señor Delgado. *Mi nombre es* Cashmere. *Hoy te voy a dar un massaje.*"

As a regular customer, Mr. Delgado knew the names and voices of all the girls, so he quickly registered the voice of a newbie, turned around to make an inspection, and was startled by this beautiful creature. Mesmerized by her radiance, he found an inability to keep his thoughts to himself and said, "Shit! You're beautiful." "¡*Diablo*! ¡*Tu eres bien buena … que linda!*"

"Gracias, Señor Delgado." Cashmere thanked him with a smile on her face that could've melted the heart of a stone-cold murderer.

"No, call me James," said Mr. Delgado. "No, no, Cashmere. *Llama'me* Jaime."

"Do you speak English?" she asked. "¿*Tu hablas Ingles*, Jaime?"

"Yes, Cashmere," he replied. "*Si*, Cashmere."

"Good … we have a new theme going on, and as you can see, I'm a sexy cop here to fulfill your fantasy. Now, get against the wall, so I can shake you down, prick," she said.

Jaime was a multimillionaire from a beautiful country who had plenty of ladies at his disposal, but he was giddy with excitement in the presence of the woman of his dreams. He'd chased her through dream land time and time again, but now she was in the flesh, so he abandoned all his inhibitions and gave her a proposition.

"I'd like for you to come work for me at my home as my personal masseuse. I'll be your only client, and I'll pay you $5,000 dollars a week … how does that sound?"

"I don't know … I'll have to think about it," she replied, as she thought the mission would be easier than expected. She knew her response was yes, but she had to stall in order to give him the impression his offer wasn't as attractive as he thought.

"I'll do it, but before I say yes, I'm telling you now, no funny business."

Shocked by her statement, he said, "Shit! All I want is your heart, sweetie." "¡*Diablo*! *Crème … lo unico que quiero es tu corazon.*"

Knowing he was full of it, she replied, "Aww, but no funny business. Now let me get to work, so I can, at least, say I worked here for a day. Now squat, lift up your sack, and cough."

\*\*\*

"Cough, cough, cough," echoed throughout the atmosphere on Spruce Street in Carwin Park. Then in his native tongue of Creole, Rob said, "This weed good. Where you get it from?"

*"Languette, zeb lo bon! Kote ou jwen seb sa'a?"*

In shock, Blizz responded by saying, "What kind of question are you asking me? And you'll have better luck finding out the color of my mother's panties before I tell you where I got this."

"Oh! *Ki kalite kesyon ou ap mande'm la? Ou genyen yon pi bon chans jwen koule kilot manman'm avan'm di ou kotem jwen zeb sa'a.*"

Irritated by Blizz hiding his punk-ass weed connect, Rob said, "To hell wit' you, and I know you got it from Swiss."

*"Myan'n pou ou! Ou jwen li nan min Swiss."*

Before Blizz could reply, they were overwhelmed by beauty. Cashmere was bad, and Blizz thought, if he hadn't met her while she was cheating on her husband, he would've made her his wife. She had beauty to spare with a mind sharp enough to cut. She was the ideal woman. As she approached the guys sitting on a park bench, Blizz shook his head in amazement because people got into relationships with expectations of them working when one of the parties, if not both, were cheating when they initially met.

"Hey, baby," said Cashmere, as she greeted Blizz with a hug and kiss.

"Is he the only mothafucka you see out here? Where's my hug and kiss?" asked Rob, making it obvious he wanted her.

"You just wanna squeeze my ass, Rob."

"You know it! That thang so soft and fat. I can't help it."

Teasing Rob, she turned to give a full view of her apple bottom that looked succulent in her fitted DKNY sweat suit, saying, "This the softest and best booty in the world," as she made it clap.

Jumping off the bench, Rob grabbed her playfully and nibbled her neck, saying, "You need to stop playin' wit' me, girl ... I'll eat you alive."

Giggling like a middle school girl with a crush, she said, "I just might let you eat me alive, but for now, it's time to get down to business."

"That's what the fuck I'm talkin' 'bout!" said Blizz, in response to getting down to business.

After sliding off from the hood to discuss current events, they ended up on the south end of town at an old school soul food eatery named Jimmy's, but it was better known as Elsie's. Over three-cheese baked macaroni, a 20-ounce steak that defined tenderness, and greens with turkey neck bones cooked to perfection, Cashmere informed them of how she started work at Jaime's home as his personal masseuse for a whopping $5,000 a week.

Once she was planted firmly within Jaime's inner sanctum, she would learn the lay of the land and report back to the Mob. After accomplishing that, she'd have his security believe they'd been misplacing their weapons on drunken nights when, in actuality, she'd be stashing them in certain sections of the house and grounds for Rob and Blizz to retrieve.

***

"Aye, Playboy ... what's good wit Rob and Blizz?" asked Divine.

"I can't call it ... I ain't heard from them niggas in a minute. The last time I spoke to Rob he was talkin' 'bout he was plottin' on a wild-ass jux and he gon holla at niggas if he need us."

"Somethin' ain't right, Playboy. I don't know what it is, but something ain't right."

"Be easy, Divine ... we good."

"Well, I'm gone, my nigga ... I'm 'bout to get up wit' my infamous head bop lady from Building 52."

"Who in 52? What floor? The Haitian one?"

"Damn! You nosey ... nah, not the Haitian one ... I call the Haitian one Caramel ... that's my lil homie, though."

"I'mma find out who she is 'cause I'mma view you goin' in the crib late night all twisted and shit ... it's cool, though ... I got a lil freak on Fairfield in Building 45 that you don't know 'bout, so we even," said Playboy.

"Whatever, nigga ... I been getting sucked off for five years, and you still don't know who it is."

"You keep sayin' 'sucked off' like you ain't fuckin' and suckin' her back."

"'Cause I ain't ... I been getting sucked off for five calendars and still ain't bust the pussy down ... that's why she's the head bop lady."

"That shit don't sound right ... that bitch twelve and you goin down, or you fuck around and be getting sucked off by a nigga," said Playboy jokingly.

"Yeah, a'ight ... she got a fat pussy that stay wet, but I be on my lazy shit when I get up wit' her ... but since you said that bullshit, I'm breakin' the routine and lettin' her ride this black platinum."

"Is she the one you call 'baby,' or is that some other bitch?"

"Yeah, that's her. I call her that 'cause, when she gets to suckin' this snake, she don't stop, like a baby on a nipple. One night, she went in on your boy all night, swallowin' nut after nut til the fourth one filled her belly."

"Sheesh! Weak niggas leave home for shit like that."

"She put in that work, my nigga ... the morning after she did that you know I hit Jimmy Jazz and Dr. Jays to cop her a fit and some Air Max 95s."

Chuckling, Playboy said, "Damn, nigga! Stop bein' stingy and shit … let me find out you don't want niggas playin' wit' your toys … you one of them get mad and bounce wit' your football-ass niggas, huh?"

"Fuck outta here, nigga … she ain't my one, so you know I ain't cuffin'. She just ain't havin' it."

***

After getting fucked and sucked into the early morning, Divine and Head Bop fell out. He was fatigued from raunchy sex and in dream land while she slept with a smile across her face. She was proud of their session because she had finally proven she knew how to work her lower back and hips by riding him like a stallion.

Divine's dream was strange, so strange he couldn't understand what was going on. What he did see clearly were two familiar faces — Robbery Rob and K-Blizz. He saw them in what appeared to be a palace, running with duffel bags slung over their shoulders, exchanging shots with their enemies. Drenched in sweat, he awoke from his slumber right before he saw the face of the person responsible for shooting both of his boys in the back of their heads at close range.

"What the fuck?" said Divine, as he surveyed the room, trying to make sense of his dream. His first thought was of the conversation with Playboy, and the words that stuck out were "Rob said he was plottin' on a wild-ass jux."

Knowing Rob was liable to be in all types of shit, he reached for both of his phones to call the duo simultaneously, but the phones kept on ringing.

Ring, ring, ring, ring, ring, ring, so he shouted, "Fuck!" and awakened his infamous head bop lady who, in turn, said, "I'd be more than happy to," as she straddled and inserted him into her love muscle.

Lil Haiti

Cashmere had been working for Jaime for about six months now, and she had earned his complete trust. He gave her the freedom to come and go as she pleased, and he made her privy to knowledge that very few had access to. She was what he thought was missing from his life, but his security team knew better and loved her because she was a sight for sore eyes and very generous with what they thought was the boss's pussy.

She solidified her position by fucking not only Jaime, but every member of his security detail. She had his hired muscle wrapped around her finger, so they promised to keep their encounters a secret at her insistence. They agreed to silence for two reasons — fear of the boss's retaliation and because she vowed they'd never get a whiff of her sweet pussy again.

In her mind, she rated Jaime's security as lames because she'd remove and stash their weapons for Rob and Blizz after every sexual encounter. They were so blinded by her beauty that the apparent was overlooked like infidelity blinded by love, so she exploited their weakness and stuck to the script.

Over the course of her six months, she stashed four semi-automatic .45 caliber handguns, three .40 caliber pistols and two Mac-10s, all equipped with silencers throughout the mansion and the estate's perimeter. She would've gathered more fire power, but she had to tread lightly during her first two months so as to not have the plan implode.

Rob and Blizz studied the blueprint of Jaime's house, which Cashmere delivered day in and day out diligently, until every detail was imbedded in their minds as if it was a home they were raised in.

During their last briefing, Cashmere informed them of the window of opportunity approaching, and about the .45 and .40 caliber handguns stashed out back beneath the fertilizer. She also told them the fertilizer was easy to locate because it was neatly stacked against a tool shed visible from the woods behind the estate, and that should be their point of entry onto the property.

"No room for mistakes, fellas," she said.

"Hold up ... thought you said there ain't a physical fence guarding the premises, but they got a motion sensitive joint that's undetectable to the blind eye?" said Blizz.

"There is, but I'll take care of that. Be on point 'cause, once the compound's power goes off and comes back on, y'all good to go ... I'm turning the power off at 11:00 pm, so be prepared 'cause this is a one-shot deal."

"You said the coke an' the bread are in two different spots, right?" asked Rob.

"Yeah, the coke is in a secret room that isn't shown on the blueprint. It's located in the pantry next to the laundry room. There will be all kinds of canned food, bread, and oatmeal inside the pantry, but don't be fooled. On the right-hand side wall, there's a canister of regular oatmeal mixed with maple brown sugars. Once you locate the regular, pull it out, and you'll find a keypad. When found, type in 443334 to open the secret room, but be cautious. Don't get locked in because the room is airtight."

"I got the powder," said Rob.

"A'ight ... I got the dough," said Blizz.

"The cash is in the study in a wall behind a custom-built fish tank. You'd never know it, but it's there," said Cashmere.

"How the fuck I'm supposed to get in the wall? You got me a sledgehammer?" asked Blizz.

"Easy ... there's a coat closet in the hallway that solves the problem. Directly to the rear right side of the wall, there will be a keypad on the floor. The keypad is located beneath a bag of golf clubs, and the code to open it is 052603. There are ten duffel bags already inside the room, so let's get it poppin'!"

"This nigga on his James Bond shit ... how you know all this shit?" asked Rob.

"Let's just say 'I'mma bad bitch'!" she said, pausing for a brief second before resuming the conversation. "I don't know if y'all are interested, but he has an arsenal underneath the garage ... check it out 'cause this is a clearance sale and everything must go ... the garage will have a Lincoln Navigator and a Range Rover waiting for you guys as your getaway cars, so let's get it."

"A'ight ... why we still here talkin'? Let's get it!" said Rob.

***

After creeping through the woods outside of Jaime's property line, Rob and Blizz, who were wearing all black attire, waited patiently for their moment of truth. Jaime's mansion was located in a remote location, and these woods separated his home from the Merritt Parkway, so the guys were at ease without the fear of nosey neighbors alerting the authorities.

The woods were pitch black, but the Mob had the advantage, which was provided by night vision goggles. The terrain was difficult to navigate, but the green visual produced by the eyewear made it a walk in the park. The eerie silence was numbing, but it was broken from time to time by the hooting of owls and the scurrying of rodents through brush. The moon was full, the wind was crisp, and their hearts raced! Rob loved a good jux, so as he waited, his blood pumped so hard that he earned himself an erection.

Ready to move on the mansion, Rob said, "Be careful, Blizz … don't hesitate to squeeze 'cause they ain't."

"I know. I know … I got this," responded Blizz.

At that moment, the lights went off, and within seconds, the guys were creeping onto the property. I love that bitch, thought Blizz, because she had not only deactivated the motion sensitive fence, she had neutralized the motion sensitive lights, also.

When they reached the tool shed, they retrieved the weapons, then split up, heading east and west.

Rob crept low by shrubs that were crafted into beautiful elephants, rhinos, and lions, but he spotted a security guard preparing a gram of coke. He was ready to inhale. Witnessing this, Rob asked himself why people paid for security when their employees were bullshitting on the job.

*Sniff* was all that was heard as the security guard inhaled a line of cocaine pure enough to cause a nose bleed. The fix was necessary to be alert, reasoned the guard, as he prepared another line and searched for tissue to wipe his nostrils. The effects of the second line hit immediately, so he attempted to recline his chair, but froze after realizing he was staring down the barrel of a firearm.

Knowing it was too late to react, the guard sat there as Rob said, "Is this what you get paid for?"

Faced with a rhetorical question, the guard remained silent, and Rob fired two shots into his forehead.

On the eastern side of the house, Blizz wasn't as subtle when he caught two guards on a smoke break. Noticing they were slipping, he ran out of the shadows squeezing, blowing a cigarette and one of the guards' jaws clean off while the other one relieved his bladder accidentally out of fear. Witness to this unexpected turn of events, Blizz laughed at the guard's reaction to the homicide, then fired three shots, one each to his head, neck, and heart.

He then ran to the pool where two other guards were in awe, watching two gorgeous girls having their way with one another with nine-inch dildos. The guards were in a trance as the girls pawed at each other, so Blizz broke them out of their lustful thoughts with a shot to each of their heads. The girls ogled one another's breasts and thrust hard plastic into each other, oblivious to the lifeless guards floating in the bloodstained pool beside them because their only concern was climaxing.

Standing off to the side, Blizz watched the girls and enjoyed them just as much as the guards. Their show was enticing, so his penis began to swell, causing him to remove his mask and approach them, asking, "Can I join ya party, girls?"

Hearing his voice, they gave him a once-over, then said, "You're a cutey, but we're strictly lickly."

Never the fan of rejection, he put his mask back on as they fondled each other and said, "It's ya loss," then fired shots into their heads.

Replaying what had already transpired, he knew that he'd fired eight of his ten shots, so he readied himself to reload. He then glanced in the direction of the dead bodies and said, "What a waste of pussy," then fired the last two of his shots into their lifeless corpses.

While all this mayhem was taking place, Cashmere was in the security booth at the entrance of the compound riding the head of security. He was in charge of the video feed monitoring the compound, and she was there solely to obstruct his view. She rode the dick like a professional cowgirl and stuffed one of her plump breasts into his mouth every time he tried to look around at the monitor.

He loved when she spoke Spanish while they freaked off, but tonight was different because she deprived him of this perk with silence due to the razor hidden beneath her tongue. He wasn't used to sharing a silent episode with her, so he asked her to talk dirty, and she did exactly that, but in English as she slit his throat while pushing his head backward. The wound opened so much that his head fell behind his back, reminding one of a Pez candy dispenser.

Her words were, "You're dead."

With six guards down, things were going according to plan as Rob lurked around the game room that was equipped with a full bar, movie theater, heated pool, and miniature golf course. In the sitting area, he spotted two guards arguing about a soccer game displayed on a wall mounted 64-inch plasma screen.

They were in such a heated debate that they thought Rob was one of their co-workers as he went behind the bar to fix himself a shot of Patrón. After taking his shot first, he refilled his glass, along with two others, then proceeded toward them. When he arrived in their immediate vicinity, he offered them the glasses, and they gladly obliged, still lost in their debate. They were so far gone, bickering about Brazil and Argentina, that they didn't notice who had produced their libations, assuming they were on the same payroll.

Having the drop on them, Rob said, "Have you seen Jaime?"

Pausing from their debate, one of them said, "He's in either the spa, Jacuzzi, or steam room. Why?"

"We have an emergency … the perimeter has been breached," responded Rob.

"Why the fuck are you in here if we have intruders?" shouted the guard, turning to face Rob.

Spotting a masked man with a silenced .45 pointing in their direction, they realized this man wasn't a comrade and shook their heads in disappointment.

"Y'all can take y'all's last shot, but put ya straps on the floor first," said Rob, and they complied, moving quickly, in hopes of having their lives spared.

"Let's toast to the good life," said Rob.

The guards were reluctant, but they followed suit, hoping rescue was on the way, but unbeknownst to them, there were only two remaining guards and Jaime left standing.

Rob then said, "Y'all already lived the good life, so it's time to die," then emptied the clip into their bodies.

Fleeing the game room, Rob headed to one of the stash spots where he retrieved a Mac-10 with a fifty-shot magazine. While locking and loading the weapon, thoughts of T-Gunz sprouted in his memory, so he smiled and moved forward.

He proceeded cautiously to the spa because he was only aware of the guards he'd taken down himself. He knew Blizz wasn't a slouch but assumed his boy had only taken out two guards so far, but that assumption berated his partner-in-crime and Cashmere.

The guard on post would prove to be a problem and hard to kill because he spotted Rob from afar and opened fire with his suppressed MP-5 sub-machine gun. The shots tore through expensive vases, paintings, and sheet rock, barely missing their intended target. Facing his first encounter with resistance, Rob ducked and cursed under his breath as the guard spoke with a heavy Spanish accent, saying, "Tonight you will die, my friend ... I am used to killing gorillas in the forests of Columbia, and you're just another monkey to me."

Incensed by the racial slur, Rob stood up and opened fire, missing his target by a long shot because the Columbian moved stealthily, thanks to his training in the military.

Approaching the corner with caution, Rob peaked, oblivious to his adversary gaining ground on him from behind. He then froze and cursed himself when he felt the barrel of the silencer against his ribs.

Knowing he had the upper hand, the guard said, "Monkeys are easy to kill! I told you that you would die." Then, he pistol-whipped Rob.

Upon impact, a loud grunt escaped Rob's throat, and he stumbled to the ground while still having a firm grip on his weapon, but the Columbian, who was trained in warfare, spotted the threat and quickly fired a shot into Rob's hand.

Dropping the gun, Rob cried out in pain, then said, "You better kill me 'cause I'mma kill you, if you don't."

Laughing, the guard ordered Rob to stand. He lowered his weapon by his side, saying, "I'll kill you with my bare hands."

"I'd like to see you try," replied Rob.

Hearing this, the guard dropped the sub-machine gun and round-house kicked Rob clean in the mouth, making him stagger. Amused, he said, "Fight back, monkey."

Spitting out blood, Rob said, "I got something for ya ass, nigga!"

Then he launched a fury of punches that were met with blocks until an uppercut stunned the guard momentarily. Seizing the moment of opportunity, Rob rushed the Columbian, but he was countered by a leg sweep that sent him flying into the wall. Bracing himself with his hands, Rob endured excruciating pain that shot through his body from the gunshot wound, so he gritted his teeth until the pain subsided.

Seeing a chance to finish off his monkey, the guard launched a barrage of kicks and punches, shedding blood with each blow.

Rob wasn't very appreciative of the ass whipping he was receiving, so he charged his assailant like a wild bull, knocking him down. Climbing atop the Columbian, he pounded with all his might. Once the guard ceased movement, Rob reached for the Rambo knife located in the Columbian's ankle holster and shouted, "I'm gonna gut you, mothafucka!" Then, he dissected him like a frog in science class.

After coming around the corner and witnessing what he did, Blizz looked at Rob with disgust, then said, "Damn! They beat ya ass, nigga!"

"He got his, though, and I'mma gut Jaime like a fish when I catch his ass," said Rob, with death in his eyes.

"Where he at?" asked Blizz.

"He in the spa."

"Let's go slump this nigga."

"Nah, you ain't ready right now ... ya hand all fucked up, so handle the powder," said Blizz.

"Bet ... I bodied four of them niggas, too," said Rob.

"Four? I slumped four, too, and I saw a guard dead in the security booth."

"In a booth? That ain't my work."

"His throat was slit, and his dick was out," said Blizz.

Without missing a beat, in unison, they said, "Cashmere!"

With nine guards down and one left, the mission was almost over, so Rob picked up the sub-machine gun the Columbian had tried so viciously to use on him, then headed to the pantry in pursuit of two hundred kilos of grade-A coke.

After easily finding the pantry, he located the canister of regular oatmeal just as easily because it stood out among the maple brown flavor. Locating the keypad, he pressed 443334. Then the trap door opened, revealing more cocaine than he'd ever seen and a scent so strong that it permeated the pantry, kitchen, and dining room. The smell of cocaine was unmistakable, so it alerted the last guard who then rushed straight for the pantry, knowing something was wrong because there weren't any transmissions on the radio indicating the door to the cocaine would be opened.

Once there, he proceeded cautiously, catching Rob in the act of filling the duffel bags. Having the upper hand in his favor, the guard said, "You might as well stop because you're about to die."

Not happy about hearing that he was going to die for the second time in one night, Rob grabbed an open kilo he had tested and threw it in the guard's face. More than a vapor went up the guard's nostrils, causing him to be blinded and sneeze uncontrollably, so the scales tipped in Rob's favor, allowing him the time to place his weapon at the guard's abdomen and say, "You might as well stop sneezing because ya about to die." Then, he pulled the trigger.

As this transpired, Blizz crept through the spa, peeking into every room he came across in search of Jaime, but Jaime was nowhere to be found. He proved to be elusive because Blizz checked the Jacuzzi, hoping to find him there, but it, too, was empty. Next, he headed to the steam room where he heard giggling coming from the other side of the door. After opening the door to take a better look, he was met with so much steam and heat that he could hardly breathe, let alone see. Tiptoeing into what felt like a furnace, he froze when he heard a female's voice say, "Right there, papi ... suck my pussy! Oooh, yes! Like that! Don't stop ... your momma should be proud of a pussy-eating mothafucka like you!"

Blizz listened carefully, trying to locate where the voice was coming from, but fog always distorted sound, leaving him clueless. Lost in the heated fog, Blizz clung to the wall, searching for the thermostat, so he could lower the temperature and gain visibility. After stumbling over the couple's undergarments, he located his savior, lowered the temperature, and stripped down to nothing but his boxers and his trusty .40 cal.

Scanning the room for its occupants, Blizz sweated profusely as he endured the heat and sexy panting of the mystery woman. Shortly after, the steam dissipated and visibility returned, revealing Jaime, ass up from behind, with his face buried in this woman's vagina. Witnessing this, he approached the couple and shot the woman right in between the eyes, killing the poor girl before she knew there was another person in the room.

Jaime then said, "Damn, mami! Your pussy is getting wetter and wetter! I can't wait to stroke it!" He was unaware of the blood pouring out of her head and down her stomach to her love.

"She's dead, Jaime! How does dead pussy taste?" said Blizz.

Frozen from both fear and disgust, Jaime said, "I have a hundred grand in my study that can be yours, if you let me live."

"Ha! Ha! Ha! I've had a hundred grand ten times over before I came in here, so what will I do with ya punk-ass hundred grand?" asked Blizz. "I'm here for the millions stashed behind the fish tank and the coke in the pantry."

Baffled by the intruder's knowledge, Jaime cursed himself because he knew the only person bold enough to divulge such sensitive information to an outsider was Cashmere.

"I'm gonna make this quick," said Blizz, as he shot Jaime ten times in the back of the head. Jokingly, Blizz then said, "I guess you earned ya red wings eating that bloody pussy."

Paranoid, Blizz headed to the closet containing the root of all evils with knots in his stomach. He moved stealthily and cautiously because he was ignorant to the knowledge of Rob eradicating the last of security. His brow, chest, and back were saturated in rivulets of perspiration. His heart thumped loudly in his chest as anticipation gnawed at him, but he proceeded onward.

Entering the closet, he moved the Armani blazers, revealing the golf clubs Cashmere had mentioned. Finding the keypad, he stooped down with his gun aimed toward the closet door just in case he encountered an unwanted visitor. Gun drawn with his right, he used his left hand to type in the combination of 052603. When the trap door opened, Blizz received the hardest erection in the world as he stared at the most money that he'd ever seen in one place in his entire life.

"What the fuck! Holy shit! This shit gotta be fake!" exclaimed Blizz, as he moved around the room, fascinated by Benjamin Franklin and Ulysses S. Grant.

"This gonna take mad trips!" he said to himself.

Sweat seeped from Blizz's pores as he filled up duffel bag after duffel bag. The stacks were heavy, but he endured the strenuous workout until there wasn't a visible green back left.

On the other side of the estate, Rob bagged kilos of grade-A cocaine into duffel bags until a room that was once white with powder was black from duffel bags.

After completing their tasks, they headed to the garage from separate directions, happier than men who had recently been released from prison. Once there, they heard one another's footsteps, then proceeded with caution because it was too late in the game to get clipped off.

Coming around the corner with their guns drawn, they stumbled upon one another by looking down the barrels of their respected pistols, so Rob said, "Put that shit away, nigga!"

Lowering his weapon, Blizz said, "We did it!"

"Yes, we did ... now let's get the fuck outta here 'cause my hand leakin'."

They took trip after trip until all the cake and coke were delivered to their vehicles, then Rob asked, "Didn't Cashmere say this mothafucka got an arsenal under the garage?"

"Hell, yeah, she did ... let's peep it and snatch what we need."

Down a flight of stairs to the right was where they found live grenades, AK-47s, AR-15s, bazookas, missile launchers, M-60s, and a wide variety of explosives.

Overly excited, they were deaf to Cashmere's foot falls as she entered behind them with her manicured fingers clutching a Heckler and Koch .40 cal. Not one to savor the moment, she fired two shots to each of their legs. Blocka! Blocka! Blocka! Blocka!

Upon impact, the guys fell to the ground and were engulfed with surprise, rather than pain, when they turned to see the face of their attacker.

While watching them squirm on the floor, she thought, How can a person trust someone who is capable of setting up another, yet whole heartedly believe it won't be done to them in return?

"You grimy bitch!" shouted Blizz.

"Nah … ya wrong about that … I'm not a grimy bitch, but I am a bad bitch," she responded, as she fired two shots, one to each of their heads.

\*\*\*

"Somethin' ain't right, Gunz," said Divine, as they strolled through the hood, looking for new pussy.

"Man … the block jumpin' with all these bitches, and you talkin' 'bout 'somethin' ain't right'? The fuck wrong wit' you? We got money, we ain't beefin', and we could fuck anything movin' through the town, so be easy."

"Chirp, chirp, chirp," rang aloud, as T-Gunz's Nextel went off, so he said, "Speakin' of new pussy ... that was a call from this new thang from down south, so drop me off at my whip. She bad as hell! Thick as a mule! She up here from North Carolina, staying wit' her people on Spruce Street, in Trinity."

"Oh, yeah? What floor 'cause I'm goin' down the hill right now."

"Nah, nigga ... I gotta bust her down first ... then I can share."

Chuckling, Divine asked, "Where ya whip at?"

"Over on G Street (Garden) on the south end."

As they pulled up at G Street, Divine got a call from a young boy who wanted a big eight (125 grams) of hard. The youngen was a half-ounce hustler who continuously fucked up money, so this was shocking to Divine. He figured the kid had caught a jux or his numerous pep talks had finally rung a bell, so he gave Gunz palm and headed to his sale.

***

"All right, guys and gals … listen up. We have a serious bust on our hands. In forty-five minutes, we will be executing a sting by the name of Operation Voodoo. Our objective today is to round up the Haitian Mob. Grab whoever you can, but our main target is the prince of the pack. He is our threat! He has the mental capacity to become a major player in these streets, so we have to get him now. These guys won't be easy to take down, unless God is on our side. Be careful, people!" said Captain Richards, speaking to a roomful of plain clothes detectives nursing Dunkin Donuts coffee.

"Okay, sir. We'll bring those no good, drug-dealing devil worshippers in today!" said Sergeant Ogden.

"Bell?" shouted Captain Richards.

"Yes, sir."

"Grab your men and prepare your strategy. You'll be in charge of the blue team."

"We're on it, sir."

"The same goes for you, Ogden. You'll be in charge of the red team."

"Yes, Captain," said Sergeant Ogden.

"Okay, team … this meeting is adjourned. Let's bring these motherfuckers in and clean up the streets of Stamford."

\*\*\*

Arriving on Orchard Street, in a section of town called the Waterside, Divine parked and allowed the young boy to jump into his vehicle. The young boy said, "What up?" as he threw $3,750 on Divine's lap. Then he said, "Hurry up, Divine. I got mad dough waitin' on me."

Divine said, "Be easy, youngen, 'cause all money ain't good money ... I see you steppin' ya weight up, too."

"Yeah, I hear that, but I'm tryna get where you at ... I need big whips, big jewels, big guns, and bitches wit' big asses ... I need to be big! Only thing is you need to practice what you preach," said the young boy, as he jumped out of the car to alert plain clothes narcotics detectives portraying construction workers of Divine's possession of crack cocaine.

"Freeze! Don't fucking move, or I'll blow your head off, you fucking coon!" yelled Sergeant Ogden, as both the blue team and his team rushed the car, catching their suspect, red-handed, in possession of an eighth of a kilo.

\*\*\*

Soaring high above the Atlantic Ocean, Cashmere indulged in a very pleasant apple martini, then said, "Hi! How are you?" to a stewardess.

"I'm fine, and yourself? May I help you with something?"

"Yes … I'm a bit nervous on planes no matter how often I fly, so would it be possible to know how much longer we will be?"

"We'll be landing at Norman Manley Airport in the tropical paradise of Jamaica in twenty minutes."

Hearing the good news, she smiled at the stewardess because she had escaped scotfree with twenty-million cash, and an added two hundred kilos that had been sent ahead of her in clothing and food containers through a friend's import-export business.

Looking at the clouds from her window seat in first class, she thought, Blizz was right. Then she whispered to herself, "I'mma bad rich bitch," and laughed.

# Chapter 3

# Four Years Later

"Wake up and get your fucking slop, you fucking coons! Chow time," shouted the racist corrections officer Neve.

"You got one more time to come out ya face," said Divine.

"I wish you would try to put your hands on me … you'd end up in the box facing a consecutive sentence faster than a pig eats shit."

"That's not a threat ... I'd rather do more time in ya fancy camp before I get deported to Haiti," said Divine, bluffing. "It'll be worth it just to take that smug look off ya face ... you ain't been through nothing. You probably never had a fight, so I know you can't stand a beatin'."

"I'll get you, boy! I swear to it!"

"I'll be waitin' to put the hand of God on ya bitch ass."

"You'll be in the hole, starving," said Neve, a little shaken up by Divine's words because it had been proven that assaulting an officer was the least of the worries on the minds of a variety of prisoners who were facing deportation to Third World countries.

"Time is time, and it'll still count, so eat a dick, cock beater."

"Man, leave that punk-ass police alone ... he ain't gonna do shit but flip ya mattress and dump all ya shit on the floor," said Rah-Rah. "Peace. They call me Rah-Rah.

What's good wit' you fuckin' wit' that pig? All he want is a nigga to put hands on 'em, so he can go out on workers' comp."

"I'm good, and they call me Divine. You right, too, so fuck that pig."

"Divine? You one of them *sak passes*."

"Yeah … I'm Haitian," said Divine, laughing.

"What's so funny, B?"

"You funny."

"How I'm funny?"

"You said I'm one of those 'what-ups.'"

Laughing, they headed to the crowded mess hall where they received white rice, black-eyed peas, baked chicken, and juice. The mess hall was filled to capacity, so the guys navigated through the crowded tables until they found an empty one where they could chop it up.

Sharing small talk in between mouthfuls of one of the few edible meals in the Department of Corrections, Divine said, "This mothafucka packed!"

"You know what it is on cheeseburger Saturdays and chicken Sundays ... there go a nigga hoppin' back in the line for seconds now ... you got some plastic 'cause I'm 'bout to cuff my bird an' bring it back, so I can season it wit this curry my man hit me off wit', then toss it in the stinger, an' eat good for tonight's game."

"I hear that ... on some other shit, though, I'm 'bout to be out ... what's good wit' you, Rah-Rah?"

"I'm 'bout to max out in a year. Then they gonna dip me back to Kingston. I coulda paroled eighteen months ago, but that damn immigration detainer popped up."

"Damn, my nigga ... you good over there? What ya locka lookin' like?"

"I'm all fucked up! My people left me for dead."

"I got a lil pull, so I'mma get you moved to 2 Buildin' wit' me tomorrow 'cause my bunky out for a work release halfway house. Once you wit' me, you be good. When I bounce, you could have all my shit."

"*Wah di blood clot? Who mi affi mek a duppy?*" asked Rah-Rah, speaking patois in full effect.

Chuckling, Divine said, "Nobody, my nigga. I like ya style. I also decided to leave you the last $2,200 in my account, so you could be good for a minute."

"Give thanks, yu hear?"

"I watch niggas, and I been watchin' you for months. I view that you a true G. I was in 5 Buildin' in the bathroom when you put that six inch in kid's eye. I'm feelin' that 'cause you rode. You ain't buckle 'cause they was deep."

During his four-year drug beef, Divine realized he wasn't doing any more jail time once he stepped back on the streets because he planned to invest his money in real estate and music. He was banking on property because it was lucrative and music because it was a passion that could produce fruit.

Months passed, and the pair of Divine and Rah-Rah were dubbed the "Caribbean Connection." They developed the bond of brothers. Then, the day of release came, when Divine heard, "Pack your shit, Jean-Baptiste. Your day has come. You look like you have a good head on your shoulders, so don't let me see you back in here," from Correctional Officer Maloney.

*** 

Once he was a free man, Divine stopped by the cemetery to see his father, Robbery Rob, and K-Blizz. He had a one-stop trip because he and the rest of the Mob decided they would have their loved ones, including themselves, buried in a mausoleum when the time came.

"Dad ... Rob ... Blizz ... I'm home now, and I'm movin' forward as a man. No more drugs bein' moved on the strength of me ... I'm tryna use real estate as a steppin' stone to have a legitimate source of income backin' the record label I want to start ... I'm bringin' T-Gunz, Young Swiss, and Playboy along for the ride, so I can keep an eye on 'em and make sure they stay outta trouble," said Divine, willing the words that poured from his core into existence. "I ain't forget y'all ... I was caught up in the system, behind the G-wall, but I'm out and will avenge y'all's deaths," he said, as he wiped a solitary tear from his cheek.

\*\*\*

"Welcome home, Divine!" shouted friends and family at his celebration.

Playboy, Young Swiss, and T-Gunz had orchestrated this gathering to help him forget about prison and to remind him of how much they loved him. Welcome Home banners and balloons decorated the interior of Club Premier. Bottles of Dom Perignon were chilled in buckets of ice. The room was filled with ladies, wearing revealing outfits in hopes of snagging a balla.

The crowd mingled and celebrated Divine's return. Fellow hustlers sent bottles because he took the bid on the chin like a stand-up man. Ladies made attempts to get acquainted with him but were discouraged when the infamous head bop lady cut in, saying, "Hi, Divine. How are you?"

"I'm good and happy to be home. Ya dig?"

"I know, I know, but enough of the small talk, Divine. I'm here for one reason and you know what it is ... can I get some of that good dick tonight? You better tell your other bitches to fall back because I got first dibs on that black platinum hanging between ya legs ... I wasn't sending you panty pics and letters and accepting calls for no reason."

"Be easy, baby … I'll let you know before the night's over."

"Don't play with me, Divine!"

"Cut it out. When have you known me to play games? You already know I'd tell you I ain't fuckin wit' you if that's what it is."

"I know but my kitty itches and only your paw can scratch it the right way."

"I'll get at you."

"You better!" she said, as she watched him walk through the crowd, looking simply delectable.

Distracted by continuous greetings, Divine bumped into a new face, almost spilling her drink, then said, "Pardon."

"Hi! How are you? Welcome home … we haven't had the opportunity to meet prior to your unfortunate situation, so don't take my bold approach as disrespect when I say, 'What the hell is wrong with you?' You look too good to be going to jail."

"Excuse me!" he exclaimed, intrigued by the beautiful specimen who had approached him in a manner he wasn't accustomed to. She blushed.

Then he said, "Let's try this again, darling. I'm Divine, and you are?"

"I'm Tessa, and I apologize if I came off sideways."

"It's nice to meet you, Tessa, and it's a'ight. If I was offended, you woulda seen the ugly side of me."

"Excuuuuse me, super-fine gangsta," she said, moving her head up and down and side to side, inspecting her target.

Divine enjoyed this little cat and mouse flirting they were engaged in, so he suggested they go onto the patio where they'd be able to talk without shouting over the music.

"Where you from, and what are ya interests, Tessa?"

"I'm from Jamaica, but I've been in this country for two years. I'm in my second year of law school at Yale University. I like to dance, read, and ride horseback, and spend time with my family. The list goes on. How about you? Besides going to prison, what are you into?" she asked jokingly.

"Ha! Ha! You got jokes. I'm into a lot of things."

"Such as?"

"I make music. I love my family. I love makin' money, and I love takin' a day off from the world sometimes, just to sit in the crib, watchin' DVDs. The list goes on."

They engaged in deep conservation up until it was around two in the morning and would've kept right on if she hadn't decided that it was getting late. She didn't want the night to end, but she knew, if she stuck around, she'd end up in his bed before the sun came up. There was an instant attraction between them, and they were aware of it, but Tessa fought the urge.

Leaving the party behind, he walked her to her car and quickly fell into a state of shock. She was a college student, so to find out she was pushing a Mercedes Benz CLK 430 was surprising. He expected to see an Accord or something of that caliber, so the shock was written all over his face.

She was very observant, so she noticed his reaction, and said, "I'm a daddy's girl."

"I bet you are," said Divine sarcastically. He then asked, "Sugar or biological?"

"What?" she asked, trying to comprehend what was just said. Hitting her, she said, "Biological ... I don't have or want a sugar daddy, asshole," with a big smile plastered on her face.

The small talk outside her car window was amusing, but it came to an abrupt stop when his phone rang. Answering his call, he placed it on mute, then told Tessa to drive safely, and he'd be in touch.

Pulling away from the curb, she said, "You forgot to ask me one question, but I'll answer it any way. I'm single, and don't forget that," with a naughty smile on her face.

Watching her tail lights fade, he took the call, saying, "Hello … what's good, Head Bop? I was just about to call you. Where you at? I'm outside the club, so come scoop me."

*** 

In Divine's native tongue, he greeted his mother, asking her how she was, "*Manman, ki jen ou ye?*"

Responding, she said, "I'm fine. How about you?"

"*Mwen byen e ou min'm?*"

He responded by telling her he was okay and was going to be walking the straight and narrow life now because he was tired of the streets and going to prison.

"*Mwen byen. Map mache S-S kounyea paske mwen bouke ak la ria e al nan prison.*"

Hearing this, Chantal, Divine's beautiful mother, looked at her son, proud he was making a change for the better. She stared at her only child for a while, feeling the sincerity in his words then spoke, saying, "Well then, my son ... you have to go to Haiti to take a shower, so all the evils and bad spirits clinging to you are chased away."

"*Se pou ou ale Ayiti pou ou binyen, change chans ou, e chase move lespri yo.*"

Allowing her words to sink in, he was quiet because he knew exactly what type of shower his mother was referring to. He thought about it for a while, then told her he agreed. He asked her to make the arrangements.

*"Dako, Manman ... range voyag la pou mwen."*

\*\*\*

*"Sak posse,* Divine?" said Tessa, in an awful attempt at saying what's up in Creole.

"Ha ha," he laughed at her butchering of his language.

He was patient and helpful with trying to help her pronounce the words and did so by saying, "It goes like this, Tessa... *sak passé?"*

"Like this? Suck pussy."

"Girl, you crazy," he said, chuckling. "You always thinking wit ya coochy. It ain't suck pussy. It's *sak passé."*

*"Sak passa passa,"* she said, as she gyrated her hips like the women in the *passa passa* videos.

"Let's try this. Say *sak* as if ya saying sock. The type of sock you'd put on ya foot."

"*Sak.*"

"Good. Now say *pas* as if you were saying the word possible."

"*Pas.*"

"You go, girl. We gettin' somewhere. Now say the letter A after you say *pas*."

"*Passe.*"

"Good. Now put the phrase together."

"*Sak passé!*" she shouted, happy that she finally got it right and that he didn't get irritated.

They became a major part of one another's lives. They had been rocking with each other for three months now, and she was a fiend for his touch. She wanted to feel him within, but she also wanted him to be hers, rather than a fling, so she made him wait it out. She knew her plan was risky because of his stature, but it was a risk she was willing to take. He had women throwing themselves at his feet, so her strategy could hit or miss. He'd either be intrigued with her and put up with the chase or say to hell with the cat and mouse and keep it moving. Fortunately for her, he was intrigued.

During their days spent together, they'd take walks through Central Park, enjoy water rides at Coco Key, the indoor water park in Waterbury, Connecticut. Compare Beardsley Zoo in Bridgeport, Connecticut, only to lean in favor of the Bronx Zoo. They engaged in live comedy shows at Caroline's Club in the city and bought each other jewels at Avianne's and Co. in the diamond district.

Love wasn't the word for what they were feeling because what they felt was euphoric, like the high brought on by E-pills. She smiled with every thought and mention of his name because she could see herself with him through her natural and after life.

He was ambitious and driven at the mast of his fledgling record label with his two partners, Mizzle the

Teacher and Maniac Main in tow, but he always managed to fit her into his hectic schedule.

Having his partners by his side made things easier because all the weight wasn't on his shoulders at all times. Their time to blow was coming real soon, so if she played her cards right, she'd enjoy the fruits of his labor because she was his baby.

***

"Damn, B! Where the fuck you been? I ain't seen you so what you up to?" asked Playboy.

"I been going to school for audio engineering at the Institute of Audio Research. I been trying to place some of our beats with established artists, been going through the legal tape of starting an independent record label, and last but not least, I been spending mad time with my shorty," said Divine.

"Hey, Gunz! Did you hear this shit? The nigga that fucked more bitches than me falling in love," said Playboy.

"Love? What the fuck is that?" asked T-Gunz.

"Leave that nigga alone! All y'all fake playas got a wifey at the crib that makes you jump when she says jump, so why y'all riding this nigga?" asked Young Swiss.

"Who jump?" asked Gunz, resenting the statement made by Swiss.

"Nigga, you wildin'!" said Playboy.

"Whatever … Gunz, you know if Ne-Ne come through right now and say 'bring ya ass home,' you'll be gone til she lets you back out," said Swiss.

"Ha! Ha! He got you, Gunz," said Playboy, keeled over, cracking up.

"What's so funny, Playboy? You can stunt all you want, but we all know you fuck with Ne-Ne's twin Mimi, and she beat niggas up, so keep on frontin'," said Swiss.

"Nigga, please … yeah, right!" shouted Playboy.

"Matter of fact, here they come," said Divine.

Hearing their girls were approaching, both Playboy and Gunz alike ducked behind Divine's Escalade, then said, "Where they at? Tell them we just slid off."

Watching this scene unfold was like watching a comedy, so both Divine and Swiss fell out, laughing at the two tough guys because the girls were nowhere to be found.

"On some real shit, Divine, you think we could make it with this music shit?" asked Gunz as Playboy nodded his approval of the question.

"I don't think! I know! What you think I invested in school for? Why you think I linked up with Mizzle out in Norwalk and Maniac Main out in Hartford? Our beats are fuego! Matter of fact, take this ride with me to Lacaye Restaurant for this Haitian food."

Wanting to know more about what he had brewing in his big-ass head, they all jumped into the Escalade that was dropped perfectly on twenty-six-inch rims by Giovanna and headed for the eatery.

Once they were on the road, Divine turned up the music loud enough to bump but low enough to talk over, so he could get their feedback on the music being played. The intro to the CD captivated everyone, then the beat dropped. The percussion was tight. The drums rocked for four bars, then the horns came in blasting through the six twelve-inch Solobaric L7s made by Kicker.

Caught in the beat, everyone nodded their heads, except Divine because he was his biggest and worst critic. The beat was tough, but he didn't like it, although there wasn't a soul who heard it that didn't fall in love with it instantly.

"Yo! Who about to jump on this shit? This shit is bananas!" said Playboy.

"Nobody. This is one of our beat CDs," he replied.

"You made this for real?" asked Playboy.

"Word to mother."

Hearing that, all three of them said, "I want in!"

"If y'all ain't down for the cause, I don't need y'all around. Y'all are like my brothers, but this ain't no game. I live this shit!! I eat, sleep, fuck, shower, ride to, and do everything to music, so I need y'all to be serious about this because there will be long, sleepless nights ahead of you."

"We with you, B. It's like starting up a new block from scratch. You could have the best work, but you gotta get the clientele to you before you start to eat. Y'all remember that? Breaking night for three hundred dollars on Lil Haiti until the block started jumping," said Gunz.

"A'ight then, I need you to go to school for film, Playboy, because ya going to do all our videos, movies, and porns when that time comes. We ain't outsourcing shit! We gonna be self-sufficient. Swiss, ya gonna start school at I.A.R to get your diploma of recording arts. Gunz, ya gonna get your master's degree in music business from Fullsail, so when we come together, we'll form like Voltron." He paused for a minute to give his words time to sink in, then said,

"Now get out my whip 'cause I gotta go see my baby."

\*\*\*

Through blaring speakers, Divine, with Tessa by his side, recorded an upcoming R&B singer's vocals, who went by the name of Sincere and whose music was heartfelt:

"You are my darling, my baby, my soul …

Girl, are you ready? If so, let's roll …

You are my darling, my baby, my soul …

Girl, together we'll conquer the world …"

Those words echoed throughout the control room, hypnotizing Tessa. She never knew how much talent Divine possessed because he'd never allowed her into the studio until that very moment.

The music was produced by Divine, Mizzle, and Maniac Main. The chorus was penned by Divine because a musical bed, along with a chorus, gave the artist a direction for the song, making it easier to complete. The remainder of the song was written by Sincere.

Everything sounded like perfection to her untrained ear, but Divine insisted that Sincere give him one more take to give the song that special feeling.

Speaking into Sincere's headphones through the talk back mechanism on the mix board, he said, "Good shit, Sincere, but I need you to hold the note on the last word of each bar. You know soul, roll, soul, and world. Hold the note a little longer for me, baby."

"A'ight. I got you."

Sincere hit it right on the head, then completed the rest of the song in two takes, so they started what would be the strip joint and club banger from his demo.

"Dip, drop, shake! Show me what ya booty makes!

Drop it to the floor and make the fellas scream your name!

This ain't a game, so, shorty, show ya g-string!

Bring it back up and shake it all again!"

"Good shit, Sincere! I could see the video now. We gonna be at Bada Bing or Sue's Rendezvous with all types of asses clappin' and jigglin'," said Divine.

"Unh-unh, you ain't about to be in no strip joint with no ass in ya face!" exclaimed Tessa.

Not feeling her outburst, he cut the music and made a screeching noise like a car coming to an abrupt stop, then said, "We can end our relationship now because I don't play that shit. You can take ya insecure, jealous ass out the door right now."

She was in total disbelief that he would talk to her in such a manner, so she stammered over her words when she said, "D-D-Divine, h-h-how could you talk to me like that?"

"Hear me out now, Tessa, 'cause I'm only gonna say this once. I'll treat you like a queen as long as you act like one, but the moment you get on some possessive, insecure, and controlling shit we're done."

"Nobody talks to me like that, Divine, and ya not about to start, so I'm gonna call my father because him a bad mon!"

"Tell him to come through, Tessa! It's about time to get my gun hot again!"

Hearing this, she stormed out the studio with her hands covering her face in an attempt to conceal her tears.

She had no real desire to have her father and her lover at war, so she reasoned that they needed some time apart.

He, on the other hand, sat behind the console, thinking nothing of the situation, because, in actuality, he wasn't wrong for setting rules and boundaries.

Breaking the silence, Sincere spoke over the loud speakers, asking, "Yo … is shorty all right?"

"She's good. It's only an emotion, so she'll get over it," said Divine.

***

It had been two months since Tessa last spoke with Divine, and she was going through withdrawals. She missed him more than a child missed its mother on the first day of school. She didn't want their relationship to be over, but she just couldn't understand why he would want to be around a bunch of naked women when he had her.

Deciding she needed a vacation, she booked a flight to Jamaica to clear her mind, figuring that she'd reconcile with him when she got back.

***

Divine was in the process of closing on two tenement buildings. He planned on making half of them section-8 approved to ensure consistent income. He had continued to live his life over the past two months, although he missed Tessa like crazy! He couldn't understand how she could be so sensitive when all he was saying was that, if she didn't trust him, there was no reason for them to be together.

He missed her, but he reasoned that things would pan out one way or another, but until that day came, he had to get his business poppin'.

*\*\**

Upon Tessa's arrival at John F. Kennedy airport in Queens, New York, she spotted a huge banner on the tarmac that read: Tessa, we're better than this, so we shouldn't let nonsense get in the way of true love. I love you.

Seeing this display of affection made her happier than a person who had just struck oil. Finding out he felt the same love for her as she did for him made her smile uncontrollably, like a kid at Christmas.

She was anxious to get off the plane, so they could share a warm embrace, but she was greeted by security when she exited the plane. One of them said, "Ms. Thomas, please come with us."

"May I ask what this is about?" she asked, curiously.

"There has been an issue with your luggage, so please head this way."

"Fine, I will! But I want to speak to your supervisor."

Boxed in by security, she was escorted to a room designed to detain passengers who were found smuggling narcotics.

"Sit here, Ms. Thomas. My supervisor will be here with you in just a minute."

"Where's the phone? I want to talk to my lawyer."

"Ms. Thomas, you're in so much trouble that the best attorneys in the world can't save you."

She wondered what it was that she could have possibly done to warrant this type of drama, so she asked herself if her father was somehow involved in this mess. He was Jamaica. He was not just a major player, but the whole island was under his control.

Reasoning that her father was a lot smarter than the American government, she abandoned those thoughts as quickly as they came.

Divine, she thought. He never complained about money, so he had to be involved in the streets. She felt like a fool because he had to have been doing dirt right under her nose. She was infuriated because she believed him when he said he was done with the streets. In mid-thought, she was interrupted when an overly tall man in an all black suit entered the room, holding what appeared to be a picture.

The tall man spoke by introducing himself, "I'm Mr. Burek, supervisor of JFK's security, and I'd like to ask you for your total cooperation."

"What's this about, Mr. Burek?"

Handing her a picture of Divine, he asked her if she knew him, and she said, "Yes. I know him. He's my boyfriend."

"Ms. Thomas, our contact tells us that you two are separated. Is that true?"

"No, that's not true! We are a happy couple!"

"You're in a world of trouble, Ms. Thomas; therefore, I would like you to answer my questions as truthfully as possible. Can you do that?"

"Yes, I can, but what is this about? Has he been in trouble?"

"I'll ask the questions, Ms. Thomas," said Mr. Burek, cutting her off.

"How long have you and Mr. Jean-Baptiste been involved?"

"Six months."

"Would you lie to protect him?"

"No."

"How do I know you're not lying now?"

"That's for me to know and for you to figure out."

"Do you love him?"

"Yes! I love him."

"Do you know the amount of time you'll get? When you're on your twentieth year, your parole officer still won't be born yet?"

After hearing this, her mouth went dry, and the room either got quiet or her thoughts got louder because all she could hear was, What did I get myself into? Who is this man? And why did I fall for him? I knew it was too good to be true.

"Since the cat has your tongue, Ms. Thomas. I'll give you a minute to gather your thoughts. I'll be back in twenty minutes," said Mr. Burek, as he exited the room, leaving her to marinate on her own thoughts.

Outside of the door, Mr. Burek instructed one of his subordinates to rush into the room, then escort her to another, so they could prepare this room for her return.

"Do you understand?" asked Mr. Burek.

"Yes, sir!" replied his subordinate.

"If she asks, tell her she's being moved for her safety … Don't mess this up because Mr. Jean-Baptiste has paid us a lot of money for this."

"Yes, sir!"

A short while later, Mr. Burek's subordinate burst into the room, grabbed Tessa by the arm, and shouted, "Come with me, Ms. Thomas!"

"What's going on?" she asked, as she was dragged to another holding room.

"This is for your safety, Ms. Thomas, and that's all I can say," said the security guard, as he exited the holding room.

In the other room, Divine, Mr. Burek, and a few members of the staff had filled the previous holding room where Tessa was held with pink and red roses. Once they were done, Mr. Burek escorted Tessa back to the previous holding room where he left her alone but not before he said, "I'll be right back, Ms. Thomas."

She observed the room which happened to be pure beauty even under her current circumstances. While waiting for Mr. Burek's return, she was surprised to see Divine, instead, when the door opened, so she said, "Divine, what's going on? How could you lie to me, Divine? I thought you were done with the streets."

"I didn't lie to you because I am done with the streets."

"But they said I was in trouble because of you."

"You are in trouble, Tessa. Ya under arrest and ya charge will be larceny in the first degree."

"Larceny? I don't steal, Divine!"

"Yes, larceny. You've stolen my heart, and that's why ya here. Do you honestly believe you'd be in a room full of roses, if you were in trouble?"

"This was all a set-up, Divine?"

"Yes."

"Mr. Burek said the roses had to be stored in here because there weren't any more rooms available."

"Who? George? He says whatever I pay him to say."

"Are you still mad at me, Divine?"

"Would I go through all of this if I was still mad? It would've been cheaper to remain mad," he said, jokingly.

144

"Boy, I hate you!"

"I hate you, too," he said, as they gave each other a long embrace.

"Do you like my earrings, Divine?" she asked, posing.

"They're nice. I hope you didn't find a sugar daddy over there."

"Shut up, boy. My dad bought them for me."

"What are they? Rubies?" he asked, as they exited the airport.

\*\*\*

Cruising through Times Square, Divine was bumpin' Sincere's demo on his way to Olive Garden, and that was when his good fortune turned to great fortune. As he sat at a red light next to a middle-aged white male in a Mercedes

Benz S65, he switched from Sincere's demo to one of his instrumentals that contained pure fire from start to finish.

The light turned green. Then he turned into a parking garage with the S65 in tow. Once there, he jumped out of his Range Rover Sport and left the door open, so his sound could ring through the garage.

Bopping his head as if he appreciated hip-hop music, the middle-aged white male emerged from his luxury sedan, then approached Divine, saying, "Hi! How are you? My name is Steven Koffski, and I represent Hot Wax records, an up and coming label that needs talented artists and producers. I'm filthy rich, so I'm doing this as a hobby. What that means is I don't want to deal with the everyday headaches of the music industry. With that being said, would you be interested in being my business partner? I'll give you a 75-percent split and full creative control. How does that sound?"

"Let me get this right. You think I'm some type of fool, huh?" asked Divine, sarcastically.

"No, sir. Everything I just told you is the truth. Here's my card. Think it over, and from there, we'll discuss business."

***

"Good morning. I have an appointment with Attorney Rysen," said Divine, as he greeted the receptionist at the law offices of Rysen and Burke.

"Please be seated, Mr. Jean-Baptiste. He'll be with you in a minute," said the receptionist.

Stepping out of his office in his expensive suit, Mr. Rysen said, "Divine, it's good to see you. What may I help you with? Did you get your big break? I hope so because that means we'll be getting paid."

"No, not yet, but a week ago, some weirdo approached me in a parking garage as I was on my way to Olive Garden in Times Square, saying he was rich and that he wanted to start a record label. He said he wasn't interested in the everyday headaches of the music business, then offered me a partnership."

"He probably is going to start a label, but it would more than likely be a very small, independent one. Do you have any CDs of your material you could leave me, so I can help shop them around? I am an entertainment lawyer, Divine. That means I'm connected. I may know people who'll love your sound."

"Yes. Here's the CD I was bangin' that night. I hear you in regards to him being honest about starting a label, but I don't see small. This guy had the swag that said 'I do everything big'! He hopped out of a brand new S65, sported a Cartier wrist watch, and flaunted an Armani suit. What made me want to slap him was when he said he'd take 25 percent and would give me 75 percent."

"Now that's a crock of shit, Divine! Nobody in their right mind would do something like that unless they were a billionaire."

"I know, right?" said Divine, as he slid Mr. Koffski's business card to his attorney.

Rysen sipped his bourbon while examining the business card, but nothing prepared Divine for what his attorney did next. Leaning back in his chair, taking a final swig of the aged liquor, he fell backward and threw his shot glass clear across the room. The name on the business card was that of a titan, so his reaction was justified. Rising back to his feet quickly, he immediately reached for the phone to dial Mr. Koffski's number.

Meanwhile, Divine sat in astonishment, watching his attorney, who was usually cool and collected, regain his composure as he dialed the number on the business card.

"Hello. May I speak to Mr. Koffski?"

"This is he. May I ask who is calling?"

"This is Mr. Rysen, from the law offices of Rysen and Burke, calling on behalf of my client Mr. Jean-Baptiste."

"Okay. I'm not sure if I really recall who that is, so refresh my memory, Mr. Rysen."

"My client says that the two of you met in a parking garage in Midtown recently, and you made him an offer regarding being your partner in an up and coming record label."

"Oh! Yes. I remember. Did he think about my offer?"

"Yes, Mr. Koffski, and his response is it would be a pleasure to do business with you."

"He's a wise man, Mr. Rysen. I'm rather busy at the moment, so I'll have my attorney contact you to go over the paperwork. Have a good day because we have plenty to come."

"What the fuck is going on, Rysen? How are you just going to put me in bed with this guy without my consent?"

"I guess it's safe to say you're unfamiliar with Mr. Koffski's financial situation."

"Okay and?"

"He owns half of Manhattan, Miami, Chicago, Los Angeles, Atlanta, and Dallas. When he told you that he was filthy rich, that was an understatement, and he's just trying to help you get rich. Music money won't affect his money. Adding music to his money will be like adding one cup of water to the ocean."

"Damn ... his money long."

"You're on your way to the top, kid!"

***

"I'd like to make a toast, so settle down, ladies and gentlemen."

"I love you, Divine," shouted a female patron who was attending Sincere's platinum party.

"I love you, too … As you all know, we're here to celebrate Sincere's breakout CD, which sold a million copies in two weeks."

The fans and fellow industry insiders had been rooting for Sincere's success since day one, so there was a round of applause while Divine shared his words.

"It couldn't have been done without Mr. Koffski, our team at Hot Wax, the drive to get it done, and the support of our loyal fans!"

There was a standing ovation from those in attendance.

"We'll continue to give you great music, so put your hands together for Sincere as he performs the number one requested song in the country and enjoy the remainder of your night."

# Chapter 4

# Present Day

"Grandpaaa!" shouted Trinity, Divinity, and Serenity, as they rushed to give their grandfather a big bear hug.

Enjoying the warm embrace, Ricardo said, "Jesus! *Mi lickle pitny dem get big*!"

"Can we go ride the horses?" asked Trinity.

"I want to go swimming. Can we go swimming, Grandpa?" asked Divinity.

"Hey, Gramps! All I want is some coconut," said B-G.

*"Look pon dem! Jesus! Mi pitny pitny get big an'*
*strong. Yu cum from foreign an' Yankee livin' so mi affi*
*teach yu 'bout yard. Yu see mi?"* said Ricardo, as he
admired his grandbabies.

*** 

Ricardo was the man in Jamaica. He'd fled the United
States twenty-five years ago after a series of robberies,
homicides, and home invasions made him a wanted man.
During his three years of residing in the United States, he'd
drifted from city to city and state to state, leaving a pile of
bodies and grieving families behind, because he loved
money and would do anything to get it.

While in the United States, he targeted drug dealers,
actors, rappers, athletes, and anybody else who looked like
they had large amounts of loose cash.

He loved Miami, Philadelphia, Brooklyn, New York, and both Stamford and Hartford, Connectict, because they all had a diverse Caribbean population, making it easy for him to blend in.

During his short three years of wreaking havoc, he had accumulated close to fourteen million American dollars, making him financially stable, but he just couldn't stop the jux. It was exhilarating, and it gave him a high that a whole forest of weed couldn't provide. He was normally the one to do his dirt by his lonesome, but he got caught in a peculiar situation, messing with a knuckle head he knew. His knuckle-head friend was a petty stickup kid who would hit up bodegas and street corner hustlers, thinking that he was getting money.

Ricardo, on the other hand, didn't move unless he estimated his vic had, at least, $20,000. Other stickup kids would say he was crazy for looking for so much in loose cash, but he would always tell them they'd be surprised by the number of people who had $20,000 or better lying around.

During his run of terror, he'd developed an affinity for rubies. This happened one day, when he was down in Manhattan's Diamond District. On this day, he spotted a middle-aged white man, who was more than likely Jewish, looking very paranoid, so he followed him until the opportunity presented itself.

Ricardo followed him for thirty blocks on foot until his mark entered a Duane Reade pharmacy. He waited patiently for his vic to come back outside, and when he did, he ducked into an alley as a short-cut home.

While in the alley, he relieved his bladder, which was full of Jamba juice, beside a dumpster, unaware of the mad man lurking near with intentions of harming him. This ended up being a fatal decision because Ricardo didn't waste any time springing to life and slapping him with the gun he held firmly.

"Don't move," whispered Ricardo.

"Take what you want. Just don't hurt me," said the vic.

"*Keep ya hand an' ya head, if ya wan see di morning.*"

"Here take this! It's one-point-five in rubies."

"Hey, idiot! *Wah yu a do wit this amount a jewelry pon yu?* Gimme dis!" he said, as he fired a shot into his vic's neck before fleeing the scene.

***

"Hey, Ricky. *Mi hear yuh a shotta,*" said Knuckle Head.

"*Hey, bwoy! Weh yuh cum from?*" replied Ricardo, insulted by this young fool.

"*Mi nah try an' disrespect yuh father. Mi jus wan show mi a true bad mon.*"

"*How yuh a go do dis?*"

"*Cum no, mon,*" answered Knuckle Head, as he walked down the 300 block of the avenue with Ricardo in tow.

If Ricardo knew this was going to be a petty bodega robbery that would have his face in the newspapers, he would've turned the other way and gone on about his business.

As they neared the bodega, Ricardo was caught off guard when Knuckle Head barged into the store, shouting commands. He only followed suit because he was a rider. Long story short, it was a petty robbery worth $2,500 that got him in a tussle that removed his mask, revealing his face to a terrified store clerk, who he couldn't kill due to police nearing the scene.

He ended up shooting and killing Knuckle Head over differences, and he also shot and possibly killed a man who had a young child with him, but he justified his actions as self-defense. Ricardo wasn't a cold-hearted killer. He would kill over money, if necessary, but he felt $2,500 wasn't worth a man's life. Before he fled the scene of the crime, he caught a glimpse of a lion head pendant that stood out because the mane was made of yellow diamonds. The eyes were black diamonds, and they seemed to be looking right through him, piercing his soul. It hung from the wounded man's neck, and he wanted to snatch it, but time was working against him, so he took off into the night.

The next morning, he saw a sketch of himself on the front page of the daily news, saying he was a possible suspect in a robbery-homicide, so he shouted, *"Bumba clot!"*, gathered his belongings, then headed straight to the airport, leaving his one-year-old daughter behind.

Once in Jamaica, he was richer than the average, so it made him some powerful political allies, who, for a small fee every month, would give him diplomatic immunity to prevent extradition back to the States.

Knowing that he had immunity, he put his murder game down to take over the island's lucrative marijuana trade. Once his competition was eradicated, he put his hustle game down, distributing 100,000 pounds of yard weed a month. He supplied the Caribbean, England, and the United States, which had an insatiable appetite for marijuana and other narcotics.

He was what some would call a "made man," who had a team that consisted of hustlers, shooters, kidnappers, arsonists, transporters, and his infamous Pum-Pum crew. His Pum-Pum crew was a team of bad bitches from Kingston, all the way to the mountain side, and everywhere in between.

These ladies were at every event the island offered. They were the forbidden fruit of the island because, once a person bit into their fruit, they were seduced, kidnapped, robbed, then led to the shooters who'd erase them from existence, then dispose of them as shark food.

Lil Haiti

Flanked by security, Ricardo granted each of his granddaughters' requests. He went horseback riding with Trinity, alongside Dunn's River. He took Divinity scuba diving in the crystal clear waters surrounding the tropical paradise. And last but not least, he taught Serenity how to climb a tree to get herself a coconut when she pleased. He spoiled them rotten whenever they came to the beautiful island, so much so that Tessa would get jealous because she was his daughter.

"Dad, can I spend some time alone with you tonight after the girls go to sleep?" she asked.

"*Everyting crisp*, dumplin'?"

"Yes, but I'm worried about my husband because he has these horrible nightmares two to three times a week. It's nothing big. I'm just a bit worried about him."

"Hmm. *Yuh seh him once a bad mon*, eh?"

"Yes, but that was the past."

"*Him probably shot a pussy dead an' him cyant live wit it.*"

"That's possible, but I think it has something to do with his father's death."

"*Weh him deh? Him cyan go check Smitty cuz Smitty big inna thee dream ting.*"

"He couldn't make it, but he promised me that he'll join me when I come next year."

"*Well, dumplin', mi cyant do nothing.*"

"I know, but I'll have him see Smitty when we come next year."

"*All right, mi dumplin crisp, so now we affi bun som ke-ke.*"

"Dad, you're too old to be smoking weed, and I don't smoke."

"*Hey, Yankee gyal, wah yuh chat bout? Granny ninety blood clot years an' she still put fiya to ke-ke,*" he said jokingly, yet, dead serious.

"Dad, you're so silly."

\*\*\*

While preparing himself for a flight to Haiti, which was long overdue, Divine's mother said in Creole, "You finally decided to take the trip to Haiti."

He responded, "These dreams are driving me crazy, so I have to go shower."

"*En fin ou deside ale an Ayiti.*"

"*Rev sa yo vle ran'n mwen fou. Pou tet sa mal binyen.*"

Landing at May Gate International Airport, he said his prayers because he was afraid of what was to come when he saw the priest that was to perform the shower ritual later on that evening. He hadn't been to Haiti since he was four, so this was to be a rude awakening for him.

The first thing that hit him was the heat. The heat was blazing because Haiti's capitol city, Port au Prince, sat between mountains that sat to the north and south. The mountains blocked the incoming breezes that rolled off the ocean.

He and his mother rode the long, bumpy ride through the rugged terrain in the back seats of a kamionet. The ride from Port au Prince to L'artibonite was longer than long, so the driver had to pull over several times for bathroom breaks. They weren't in America, so they didn't have the luxury of truck stops; therefore, the bathroom was wherever a person pulled out or squatted.

When they finally made it to town, they saw the everyday hustle and bustle you would see in any city. The only difference between L'artibonite and Port au Prince was that L'artibonite was the country, and Port au Prince was the city.

As they traveled through town, he was saddened by the living conditions in which some of the people lived, so he gave those who he felt were the neediest $100 US which was equivalent to $375 Haitian dollars.

As he did his good deeds, he overheard voices in the background say, "He's an American Haitian."

"*Sa se yon djaspora wi.*"

Shortly before they arrived at the priest's house, Divine noticed that it stood out from the remainder of the neighborhood. It resembled a colonial in New England, rather than the brick structures he'd seen thus far, so his eyes were locked onto it. From the outside looking in, one would think he was walking aimlessly, but he was completely aware of his surroundings, so he heard clearly when people spoke about him.

One person said, "He looks like Alix. They could possibly be related," while the other said, "He's going to handle his affairs since he's going to the priest's house."

*"Li samble ak Alix. Ou si ke yo pa fanmi?"*

*"Li ap fe sa li dwe fe paske li prole kay hougan'an."*

He was more than apprehensive, but once he entered the house, the priest knew his name and the reason for his visit. Assuring him that all would be fine, he told Divine to go into the bathroom, remove his clothing, and stand in the bathtub.

New to this whole ordeal, he hesitated after the priest gave him the instructions to remove his clothes. He sensed Divine's fear, so he said, "The only way your dreams will stop is when you chase away the evil spirits."

*"Sel fason pou rev sa yo sispan se le ou chase move lespri yo."*

After making the decision to go all in as if he was playing poker, he took off his clothes, then stood in the bathtub and awaited the next instructions.

In the tub beneath him was a bucket full of murky water and leaves that he examined with the utmost curiosity. Entering the bathroom, the priest told him to lather up with a bar of soap, then use the murky water from the bucket to rinse off.

He did as he was told and was surprised to see that the water was room temperature. It made him feel dirty because of the leaves in it and when what felt like salt stuck to his body. Once he was done, he was told to let his body air dry and to face the priest, who then said his cleansing prayer while blowing cigar smoke to the north, south, east, and west of Divine's body. He then gave the cigar to Divine and instructed him to blow the smoke to the north, south, east, and west of himself while he stood behind him, saying a prayer.

After thanking the priest, he got dressed, then proceeded to leave, but the priest stopped him to give him a silk handkerchief that was meant to keep him safe. Once outside, Chantal told her son that all would be well, as long as he believed so. Hearing her out, he took her advice, then asked her for his grandfather's name.

"His name is Alix Jean-Baptiste. Why?"

"When we got here, I overheard somebody say that I look like Alix and that we could possibly be related."

"Baby, I've never met him, so I don't know. All I know is what I heard in stories."

"What have you heard?"

"Let's just say, your grandfather is a very mystical person that a lot of people fear and respect."

"I want to meet him."

"I wouldn't know the first place to look on this island of seven million people."

"Where there's a will, there's a way," he said, as he searched for the lady who said he resembled Alix.

Scouring the block, he spotted the older woman, then spoke in his native tongue, saying, "Excuse me, mommy. Can you help me find Alix? He's my grandfather." *"Eskize'm manman eske ou ka ede'm jwen Alix? Li se gwan papa'm e mwen ta rin min rankontre li."*

The lady was startled when she heard him speak Creole. After getting over her surprise, she said, "My child, you speak Creole? Alix comes around at night and be careful when you see him." *"Petit mwen ou pale kreol? Alix vini la'a le swa e fe atansyon le ou we li."*

Taking heed to her words, he gave her a thousand US dollars, then said, "Thank you," and she hugged him with so much excitement you'd think he'd just proposed to her.

*"Mesi, manman."*

Chantal was a bit skeptical about this meeting, but he was a grown man who made his own decisions, so she said nothing and just followed suit.

Nightfall came, and the streets were pitch black from a lack of running electricity. The only things that supplied light were candles and the headlights on passing cars.

Divine was a man on a mission waiting patiently. Throughout the night's silence, he heard subtle conversations and music by Sweet Mickey, but he didn't see Alix. He was on the verge of becoming frustrated, but at that moment, a Nissan Pathfinder pulled up playing conga drums that could hypnotize. The rhythm from the drums seeped into his soul, so he unconsciously began tapping his feet and rolling his hips. The music brought him into the path of the 4x4s headlights, and this proved to be a very peculiar situation because he found himself singing along to a song he'd never heard before, a song that the average Haitian ran away from.

Seeing this, Alix said, "Little boy, do you know who I am and what master I serve? How do you know this song, and why do you look so familiar?"

"*Ti gason ou kon'n ki moun'n mwen ye e ki lwa'm sevi? Ki jen ou kon'n chante sa'a? Ou samble yon moun mwen konin.*"

Hearing this from who he assumed to be Alix, he did not respond but kept singing the words to the song:

"Dambala is the spirit of snakes.

Dambala is the spirit of snakes; give her syrup (something sweet).

*Dambala se lwa koulev la ooo.*

*Dambala se lwa koulev la bali siro.*"

Watching this young man, Alix saw something he liked. He liked the fearlessness that he saw in Divine, so they sang the rest of the song together:

"To follow, they'll follow me here.

They'll follow me ooooo.

It's me *Ayida Wedo ooooo*.

It's me *Dambala Wedo ooooo*.

They haven't seen when I turn into a snake ooooo.

*Pou swiv, yape swiv mwen la'a.*

*Ala yape pou swiv ooooo.*

*Se mwen min'm Ayida Wedo ooooo.*

*Se mwen min'm Dambala Wedo ooooo.*

*Yo po ko we kote'm tounin koulev ooooo."*

When the song came to an end, Alix asked Divine what his name was, and he responded with both his first and last name. He automatically knew who Divine was because he'd seen him in the hospital during the week of his birth. That was his first and last time he'd seen his only grandchild up until now. He'd heard that he had a grandson when his son Joseph called him, so he flew to the States to meet his grandchild. When he made it to the hospital,

172

Chantal was asleep with baby Divine resting on her chest. This had taken place twenty-nine years ago, but the memory was fresh in his mind. On that night, he greeted his son, who then picked up and handed Divine to him.

He hugged Divine snuggly as he said a silent prayer of protection for him. Once his prayer was done, he whispered the words of Dambala's song to baby Divine, then said, "The spirit is a part of you, so you'll always be able to find me when you need me."

He then gave the baby back to Joseph. Then they strolled down memory lane for a while. The conversation was light and full of humor, but Alix ended it early in fear of waking Chantal.

Before exiting the hospital room, he gave his son a hug and his grandson a kiss on the forehead, but not before saying, "This country is freezing," although it was August.

Now that they were meeting in person again, he asked Divine how he was and what had brought him to

Haiti. He replied, saying that he was okay and that he was in Haiti to take a cleansing shower.

Hearing these words come out of his grandson's mouth made him crack a smile and laugh because he was surprised he knew about such a thing since he had been raised in the United States. It was a surprise, but he quickly came to the conclusion that his mother had advised him to take the trip, and he was right because she appeared from the shadows at that very moment.

"How are you, Chantal?" asked Alix.

"Oh, you speak English! I'm fine, and yourself?"

"I'm okay. Actually, I'm happy to see my grandson."

"Well, there he is."

"What are you looking to gain by taking a shower, Divine?" asked Alix.

"I'm trying to get rid of evil spirits."

"Why? What's bothering you? Is there someone after you?" he asked, on the defensive, ready to protect his grandson.

"No, nothing's after me. I came because I have nightmares almost every night."

"I see. I guess it's safe to say these nightmares are directly related to both your father's and your two friends' deaths."

The words of his grandfather took him by surprise, so he looked at his mother in shock while she returned the same look of bewilderment. Baffled by his grandfather's info, he asked,

"How'd you know that?"

"I may have not known what you looked like, but I've followed your life through the spirits. We are connected, my son. We've been connected since you were an infant because I came to the hospital when you were a newborn. I held you in my arms and asked my master

Dambala to keep you safe and to treat you as her own. How do you explain that you were able to recite a song you last heard when you were only a few days old?"

"Speak to Dambala for me. Ask her to show you who killed Dad, Rob, and Blizz."

"I know who killed my son and your friends, but this is your mission. You're out for your own retribution, so I can't interfere. I'm a powerful man because I serve Dambala, and I could've squashed the man with the rubies a long time ago by pulling a star from the sky while saying my prayer. Once I returned the star back to the sky, he'd drop like a fly. I haven't done so because you have to complete this task."

"How do you know about the rubies?"

"Do you honestly think I wouldn't know who killed my only son? If something were to happen to you, I would have no choice but to kill the bastard that killed my son."

"What's his name?"

"I can't tell you, but I will say rubies affect you in a strange way, so don't wear them or have them around you before you lay down to rest."

"I'll remember that, but what about the person who killed my friends?"

"Let's just say, when you find one, you'll find the other because they go hand in hand."

"Thank you, Grandpa Alix."

"One more thing, your enemy is closer to you than you think."

\*\*\*

"Divine, honey, we're back, and I can't wait to tell you how much fun the girls had with my father," said Tessa.

"Daddy, we're home!" yelled Trinity and Divinity.

"Dad, where you at?" asked B-G.

There was no response, so they assumed he was in the studio, mastering his craft of music making. Figuring he was home, the girls went to their separate rooms to unpack as Tessa made her way to their lovely home's east wing in hopes of finding her husband in his recording studio. Upon entering the studio, she noticed it was empty, but she did find a note attached to the computer's monitor that read:

Hey, baby. I know you're going to be mad I didn't go to Jamaica with you and the girls, but I had to go to Haiti instead. There is a family emergency that I need to attend to, so I'll be home the day of or after your return. Love, Divine. P.S. Kiss the girls for me.

After reading his letter, she got hot as her blood simmered to a boil. He could go to Haiti at the drop of a dime, but he couldn't find his way to Jamaica with his family.

"I'm going to fix you, Divine! You're going to sleep with your dick in the desert for the next two weeks," she said as she stormed out the studio with vengeance on her mind.

*** 

"Tessa, I'm home!" shouted Divine, as he dropped his luggage on the marble floor to his foyer.

His nose flared from the aromas of Tessa's rice and peas, stew chicken, and peanut punch as he headed toward the dining room. As he approached the dining area, he heard the girls talking, but that came to a stop when they spotted him. They rushed him, knocking him off balance, saying, "Daddy, we missed you!"

"We had so much fun, Daddy!" said Trinity.

"Gramps is so cool, Dad. He can climb a tree faster than a monkey," said B-G.

"I saw all types of fishies when Grandpa took me *scooby* diving, Daddy," said Divinity.

Laughing, he said, "It's called *scuba* diving, not *scooby* diving, Divinity ... and I'm happy to hear you enjoyed yourselves."

Tickling Divinity, he said, "I'm coming with you next time, so we can go *scooby* diving," as she squealed in delight from his touch.

He hadn't heard a peep out of Tessa, so he knew she was upset; therefore, he tried his hand at flirting with her by saying, "Compliments to the chef because the food smells good and the chef looks better."

"Don't play with me, Divine, because I'm not your friend," she said.

"Tessa, cut it out. We can talk about whatever it is that's bothering you tonight because now is the time to eat."

"Oh, I'm sorry, honey. I didn't fix you a plate because I didn't think you were a part of this family. If you want to eat, the plates are in the cupboard," she said, as she sat down to say grace.

He'd expected her to be mad, but he didn't like what she said about him not being a part of the family. He respected her feelings, so he sucked it up but would address it later for sure.

***

"How was Haiti, honey?" asked Tessa sarcastically.

"It was okay, under the circumstances," he replied.

"What was so important that had you leave on a whim?"

"Tessa, I don't want to fight with you. I want to make love to my beautiful wife, who cooked my favorite meal, who looks good in her silk negligee right now, and who I know tastes great," he said, as he nibbled on her collar bone.

Still angry with him, she shut down his sexual advancements quicker than a parole officer violating a client who had just been picked up for a home invasion.

"That was cute, but you didn't answer my question, Divine."

"The truth is that I went over there to put a stop to my nightmares. You don't know this, but the night you left, I woke up crying from my nightmare."

She hated his recurring nightmares just as much as he did, so his words touched her, but she still wasn't his friend. She figured she'd make him sweat for a day or two before she'd let things go back to normal. She asked, "What did you find out in Haiti?"

"I found out I have a grandfather by the name of Alix, who is extra-mystical. I found out the shower my mother wanted me to take isn't bad at all. I found out rubies affect me in a strange way, so I can't be around them for long periods of time or right before I go to sleep."

"Rubies? That's some Haitian mumbo jumbo! My favorite earrings are encrusted with rubies!"

"Well, take them off, so I can nibble on your ear."

"Boy, stop! You're not getting any of this wet-wet tonight or tomorrow, and I guess we're gonna see how well you deal with rubies because my father just gave each of the girls a pair of ruby earrings."

"Unh-huh, yeah, now bring that big ole thang over here," he said, ignoring her due to being preoccupied with kissing and licking her inner thigh.

"Boy, stop! You know that's my spot. Please. Stop. Don't," she plead, as he licked all the right spots.

Slipping his tongue inside her love canal made her sing another song where the lyrics were the same but in a different sequence. At first, she sang, "Please. Stop. Don't." Then she sang, "Please don't stop," into the early morning.

# Chapter 5

# Six Months Later

"Good morning, ladies," said Divine, in an overly good mood as he kissed his wife and daughters at the breakfast table.

."Good morning, Daddy," said the girls, followed by a "Good morning, daddy," from Tessa, who had a glow on her face from last night's sexercize.

"Mommy, you're silly. He's not your daddy," said Divinity, giggling unaware of the context in which "daddy" was used.

When her words seeped into his mind, he blushed because he loved being able to please his woman in all aspects — emotional, sexual, and physical.

It was a good day in the Jean-Baptiste home. The girls were off to Divine's mother's house, Tessa was off to the salon to get her hair and nails done, and Divine was left alone for what he called "me time."

Having his home to himself, he could've run around the house butt naked, made some music in the studio, and went over his taxes or anything else he wanted, but he opted to reflect on the last six months of his life since he'd returned from Haiti.

He sat around the house counting his blessings because he hadn't had any turbulence in his marriage, his daughters were healthy, and he was wealthy. Last but not least, he hadn't had a nightmare about his father or Rob and Blizz since he'd placed foot on the magical island of Haiti.

He felt all his problems were taken care of because he hadn't seen Tessa or the girls wearing those dumb-ass ruby earrings. The label was doing great, and his tenement buildings were always filled to capacity, awarding him a nice profit monthly. Topping it off was the fact that he was young and able to enjoy the fruits of his labor.

His thoughts were everywhere, but he spoke aloud, asking, "Why does Tessa like those earrings so much?"

Besides being a gift from her father that held sentimental value, he didn't see what there was to like because he honestly thought rubies were ugly. As quickly as the thought escaped his mind, a new one popped up, making him remember the conversation he'd shared with his grandfather back in Haiti.

The words were: "Rubies affect you in a peculiar way, so don't wear them or have them around you before you lay down to rest." The words echoed through his head, making him shout,

"Oh, shit! It can't be! I gotta be buggin'!"

He had an idea but wanted to see if his hunch was correct, so he called Tessa to tell her that he was taking her out to dinner later on that night.

"What's the special occasion?" she asked.

"I don't have a special occasion. I'm doing this just because."

"Do you mind if I ask where you're taking me?"

"Nothing fancy. We're going to Sammy's in City Island."

"Divine, you know that's my spot! You must want to do something freaky afterward because you know you drive me crazy when you're sucking on crab legs."

"You already know ya gonna be my dessert, so wear your ruby earrings because I bought you an edible thong that matches them."

"Boy, you nasty," she said, jokingly.

"And you love my nasty ass."

"I'll see you when I'm done here, honey."

"Later."

Now that his plan was in motion, he was anxious to put his tongue and dick game down to put her to sleep by his side.

***

After a night of good eating, drinking, and conversation, they left Sammy's and headed home, flirting and cuddling like newlyweds. Pulling up at a red light, she sat silently in the passenger seat, feeling frisky from the effects of Dom Perignon Rosé. Her mind was consumed with lust, so she pulled up her dress and spread her legs to reveal her love muscle that wasn't concealed by panties. Watching this through his peripheral, Divine realized what she was saying. Before he could join to engage in what was on her mind, a light rain began to fall, giving him an idea.

She was completely comfortable behind the dark tint of his Escalade, so she began to rub her swollen clitoris slowly and sensuously, opening a flood gate of juices into her love canal. He, on the other hand, remained quiet, watching his baby grind her love into her fingers while searching for a parking spot at Scalzi Park. He was totally aroused by her actions that he had an erection that could jack hammer through concrete. Aware of his watchful eye, she inserted two fingers into her wet pussy, then slowly took them out to place them in his mouth while asking,

"How does this pussy taste, daddy?"

He loved her juices, so he sucked on her fingers the way a bear did when their paws were drenched with honey, then said, "Hmmm … finger-licking good, bae."

Excited and ready to make it happen, he threw the truck in park, then leaned over to gently place kisses on her love. His soft lips made her reel with anticipation, so she arched her back, thrusting her hips upward to give him a mouthful of her fat, juicy coochy.

Her love dripped from his sensual touch, so he knew she was hot and bothered, and for that reason, he licked hesitantly with the tip of his tongue, as if he was trying a foreign food for the first time.

She knew he was playing with her, but she was determined to get hers, so she placed her feet on the dashboard, then put her sex in his face. Seeing that she really wanted it, he continued to tease her, only stopping to ask, "Is that how you like it?"

She replied, "You know how I like it, so don't play with me, daddy."

Loving that she was horny, he said, "If you want it, you gotta come get it," as he stepped out the truck and into the rain and the night's chilly air.

Standing in front of the Escalade, he motioned for her to come join him in the rain, so she removed her dress but remained in her heels as she exited the vehicle. The raindrops beaded up on her hourglass frame, making her look like a goddess, so butterflies fluttered in his stomach from anticipation. She wanted him badly, so she approached with a strut that a runway model would kill for. Her firm thighs melded into her well-defined calves, her flat, taut stomach, which complemented her perfect-sized breasts, and her wide hips made any nigga walking toward her automatically say she had a fatty.

Walking toward him with animal lust in her eyes, she placed her arms around his neck, then gave him an aggressive kiss that only said desire. Their lips were locked for an eternity as he squeezed her fat ass with one hand, while she eagerly removed his clothes to gain access to his manhood.

The rain started at a light drizzle, but now it came down hard, making them more aggressive with one another. The rain was the call of Mother Nature, so he placed her on the hood of his truck, then spread her lips, revealing her mother pearl.

He licked her as if he would win a prize for an outstanding job. Licking her from hole to hole along with the night's chill and rain had her on cloud nine. He feasted on his wife's love, licking and slurping that coochie like a nigga out in the cold with a cup of Oodles of Noodles. She was in ecstasy, nearing climax, rubbing his bald head, so she grinded her pelvis into his face as she shouted obscenities, "You slick tongue, nasty, pussy-eating mothafucka! Ooooh! Suck that pussy!"

Enjoying that he was pleasing his woman, he became more aroused, licking her clit with his precise technique. He then inserted one finger into her vagina, scratching her g-spot by doing the come here motion all while slowly fingering her ass with the other hand.

She was in heaven, stuttering over her words, "Oh, shit!"

"Oh!"

"Oh, shit!"

"Don't!"

"Don't!"

"Oh, shit!"

"Shit!"

"Don't stop!"

He then propped his elbows on the hood of the truck, holding her up in the air as if he was about to drink from a soup bowl. She came hard from the maneuvering of his tongue, then went limp in his hands. She was far from over, so he began to slowly kiss her inner thighs, stomach, breasts, and lips to wake up the sexual demon that hid beneath her skin.

Descending, he traced circles around her belly button before pushing her knees to her shoulders, exposing her anus. Her opening peeked at him, so he licked her thoroughly, creating goose bumps all over her flesh.

"Oh, shit! What are you trying to do to me?" she asked, as he continued to do his obligatory job of pleasing his woman.

The rain now went from hard to a torrential downpour, but he positioned himself to enter her cavern of love. Entering her slowly and to the depths of her tunnel, he proceeded to grind into her love, rolling his hips in a circular motion. She begged for more of his touch while spreading her legs as far open as possible to allow him maximum penetration. He stroked and stroked as she pinched her own nipples, which were oh-so-sensitive from the tingling sensation caused by the downpour.

Her moist, velvety vagina felt remarkable, so he spoke through clenched teeth, saying,

"Damn! Ya pussy good to me! You got my fit, love! This pussy like O.J.'s glove."

Loving the compliments and the rhythm of his thrusts, she came again with a shiver that had nothing to do with the cold rain.

The pussy was good no matter the position, but he roughly turned her around, then slapped her ass. He entered her quick and hard while she held the grill of the truck for support. She took the dick like a pro while throwing it back in sync with him, making a clapping sound.

Clap, clap, clap, clap.

He threw his cock into her stomach while holding her tiny waist with one hand and a breast with the other. He pounded deeper and harder, only letting go of her breast to grab her hair. Clenching a fistful of hair, he pulled her head back, so he could suck on her neck and ears while whispering, "This my pussy! You better not ever give it away."

"It's all yours, daddy. I'm your freak bitch, and your pussy is safe. You're my nasty nigga that gets the job done every time. I love you!"

"Bae, I'm 'bout to cum … you gonna catch it?"

"Just say the word, and I'll catch every drop in my mouth, daddy."

"Oh, shit! I'm cummin'!" he said, as he spun her around by her hair, so she could make good on her word of catching every drop.

Without hands, she navigated his cock into her mouth where she deep throated him until he exploded, releasing his children down her throat. She enjoyed swallowing his kids for two reasons. One being that she let the freak out to keep her man satisfied. Secondly, because every man has swallowed his girl's cum when he was face first in between her legs.

Exhausted from their workout, they stood in the rain for a while, then retreated to the safety of the SUV, where they reclined their seats, and stared at each other for a job well done. The feelings coursing through their bodies gave them a sense of euphoria. Although they had been married a while, the fire burning between them still blazed strong, and tonight it showed. Too tired to move, they sat in the Cadillac, thinking to themselves, My baby the truth, and I love 'em. Then drifted off to sleep.

***

The following morning, Divine jumped out of his sleep, then said, "Shit ... I was right."

Realizing his theory about the rubies giving him nightmares was correct, he decided to take a trip to see if the second part of his theory was correct. Unwilling to lie to Tessa, he stretched the truth, telling her he was taking a quick trip to film a music video for one of the artists on the label.

In response, she asked, "Where will the trip be, and how long will you be gone?"

"Negril, and three days," he said, nonchalantly.

"Negril … are you trying to tell me that you can go to Jamaica for a fucking music video but are always unavailable to go with your fucking family?" she shouted, extremely angry with her husband of seven years.

"I knew you were going to act like that, but I still came to tell you, rather than hide the truth. Besides, I'm going to Jamaica with you next year."

"Negril … you ain't slick, Divine."

"What are you talkin' 'bout?"

"I'm talking about Negril, mothafucka! Hedonism 2 is in Negril!"

"This is a video shoot, not a weekend retreat with my mistress."

"I want you to cancel this video, Divine."

"That ain't goin' down, Tessa."

"Are you going to put this video before our happiness?"

"Our happiness? This video and countless other videos are the reason you're happy, living in this house, driving those European cars, and wearing those diamonds, so this discussion is over."

"If you walk out that door, I won't be here when you get back," she said to his back because he was already out the door.

Pulling out of his driveway, he dialed a number on his cell phone. It rang three times, and the person on the other end responded, "Hello."

"What's good, homie?" asked Divine.

"I'm good, and you?"

"I need a small favor from you, but I'd like to know if ya up to it before I tell you what it is."

"For you … anything!" said the mystery man on the other end of the phone.

"Good … I'll be waiting for you at the Subway on the corner of Mrytle and Elm."

***

Speaking in his native tongue of Patois, Rah-Rah told his sister that his boy was coming to Jamaica from America, so have a female friend for him. "Hey, Tasha, *mi brethren cum a yard from foreign, so have a gyal fi him.*"

"A who?" she asked.

Getting serious real quickly because he had genuine love for Divine, he spoke without his Jamaican accent, saying, "My brother, the only person that was there for me when I was locked up, even though I had a blood-related sister by the name of Tasha out doing her own thing. She was out doing God knows what during my time of need."

"Hey, *bwoy, stop yuh cry*," she said, offended by his statement because it was true.

"*Cry, when mi have no money fi eat, him alone feed di dog. So if him seh murda a pussy ole mi affi shot him dead!*"

"*When him a cum?*"

"*Tree day!*"

"*Cool it no mon. Mi have a gyal fi him.*"

"All right ... *everyting crisp.*"

***

Sitting at a table in Subway, Divine waited for his mystery friend while eating a foot-long turkey and cheese sandwich with extra jalapeños. When this mystery friend arrived, he ordered a Coca-Cola soda, not for taste but as a chaser for the white rum in his army jacket's top right pocket. Sitting across from one another, he offered Divine a shot of rum, which he accepted eagerly. They went down memory lane and caught up with each other over turkey and rum. It had been a while since they'd last seen each other, but they were closer than brothers. The mystery man was addicted to the street life, so Divine offered him a position in his company to give him a shot at walking the right way, but he just wasn't ready to call it quits. His offer was open-ended, so there would be a position open whenever he was ready to go legit. After twenty minutes of small talk, they got down to business. Divine said, "I need you to do a snatch and grab at this address when I call, but only if I call to give you the go."

"What the fuck? Do you know what address you just gave me?" asked the mystery man, as he read the napkin containing the address.

"Yes, but I don't want anyone to get hurt. Just make sure everything goes smoothly."

"Are you sure?"

"Yes, I'm sure but go only if I give the go."

\*\*\*

"Bumba cloooot!" shouted Rah-Rah, as he greeted Divine at the Norman Manley International airport in Jamaica.

"*Sak passé?*" asked Divine, as they gave one another a big, bear hug.

"What brings you to the island, Divine?"

"I wanted to see my boy, plus make sure it was safe to bring my family out here next year since I heard there was a dangerous guy named Ricardo out here runnin' the island."

"Who? Ricky? *Mi know him. Him cool wit mi sister.*"

"Are you talkin' about the same sister that left you for dead when you was up north?"

*"Yeh, mon. Dat mi sister an mi cyant turn mi back pon her."*

"I feel you."

*"Dat a wicked lion head, my yout!"* exclaimed Rah-Rah, admiring Divine's necklace which was flooded with yellow and black diamonds.

"You like it?" he asked, as he reached into his Louis bag to retrieve a scorpion encrusted in white diamonds. He then handed it to Rah-Rah, saying, *"Dis fi yu mi brother."*

*"Bumba clot …* give thanks, *yuh hear?"* he said, as he placed the necklace around his neck.

After escorting Divine to his Mercedes E-500, he took off through Jamaica's narrow streets while telling him what was happening on the island.

*"Di bwoy yuh hear name Ricky run tings. Him have ke-ke, coke, pum-pum, an' di machine dem wit x-amount a shotta fi fiya dem, but still him cool. Mi sister run him Pum-Pum crew."*

"What's the Pum-Pum crew?"

"*Di crew, dem a bag a pretty gyal who affi find any bwoy wit money an' set him up.*"

"Son ain't playin' no games, huh? He wants to get it every way possible."

"*Yeah, mon ... dem seh him mek ten million blood clot dollar a month!*"

"Got damn ... that mothafucka eatin'!"

"*Di dog him feed ... dem bwoy deh ... Pure shotta!*"

"I want to meet him, Rah-Rah. You think you can make that happen?"

"*Wah type a business yuh have wit' him?*"

The car grew silent for a while as Divine thought about a response until he eventually said, "I'm lookin' for a reggae artist."

"*Hmmm. Dat nah sound too convincing, my yout ... Beside him shotta, him have Smitty. Him deal wit pure*" *obiah, so if yuh nah have good intention he a go feel di vibe."*

*"Nah, nah. I need a reggae artist from di gully side."*

*"Really an' truly, if yuh hav bad intention, Smitty will know."*

Putting on his Jamaican accent, he said, *"Cool yuh self no, mon. Everyting crisp."*

"All right. *Now yuh affi meet mi sister Tasha an' di Pum-Pum crew."*

"I'm not fuckin' with none of them bitches for two reasons. One bein' I ain't creepin on Tessa. Two, them bitches grimy."

*** 

In an undisclosed location on the island, Smitty had candles lit and incense burning while conducting his ceremony. He poured rum on the floor to the north, south, east, and west of the room as an offering to the spirit he served. He did a prayer thanking the spirit for everything it had done to protect him, Ricky, and the organization. After thanking the spirit, he asked him his regular questions, and they were, "Do you have any police investigations on us? And is there anyone close to us that would like to harm Ricky?"

Possessing his body, the spirit spoke through him saying, "My son, you have no investigations because you move right and you pay the police good money. Police and informants aren't your problem. Your problem is a man out for vengeance, but I can't tell you who because he's protected by a powerful spirit ...What I will say is, 'be careful.'"

Those were the last words the spirit said before it picked up the three-quarter full bottle of rum and threw it back straight without a chaser.

"Make sure you have more rum before you call me because I won't show up next time if you don't have, at least, three bottles," said the spirit, exiting Smitty's body.

The spirit used his body as a vessel, then fled, but he didn't have any aftereffects from the rum, even though it was consumed by his body. Now that he was alone again, he felt a vibe that sent chills through his entire being. Unaware of what to do or say, he picked up the phone to call Sleepy, Ricky's head of security, then said, *"Security pon Ricky extra blood clot tight tonight!"*

\*\*\*

The music coming out the speakers at Reggae Sun Splash was deafening, and it was a star-studded event, featuring artists such as Beenie Man, Buju Banton, Elephant Man, and old timers like Barres Hammond, Sizzla, Luciano, and more.

To the left side of the stage was a stable of stallions, dancing and gyrating their hips. These were some of the baddest bitches Divine had ever laid eyes on. They attracted attention from both straight and homosexual men. Women couldn't resist them either. Rah-Rah noticed what had Divine's attention when he didn't notice the pretty brown-skinned thing backing her big ole ass up in front of him, so he asked, *"Yuh see di one inna di middle?"*

"Yeah, she tough, Rah."

*"Dat mi sister Tasha an di rest a dem gyal deh Pum-Pum crew."*

Rah-Rah's words sunk into his mind while thinking that every one of them were bad. He now understood how they ended up getting so many niggas got.

*"Cum, mek mi introduce yuh mon."*

Leading the way, Rah-Rah brought him to a flight of stairs that led to the rear of the stage. Boarding the stage, they appeared behind the girls, and there was booty everywhere. Pointing to each of the girls, Rah-Rah said their names, saving the best for last. The one he saved for last had the biggest ass this side of the galaxy! Divine was in awe, transfixed on how her ass swallowed the lime green thong she wore underneath nothing but a white fishnet outfit. As Divine's manhood began to rise, Rah-Rah said, *"Dat a di one dem call di boss' wife.* Her name is Cashmere an' she Spanish, but *she a yard long time."*

"Let me guess, you're talking about Ricky when you say the boss."

"Correct, *my yout. Yuh see him deh?"*

"Where?" he asked, but before Rah-Rah could answer, he spotted Ricky on the stage, seated on what appeared to be a throne, surrounded by security and Jamaica's elite.

Completely aware of his surroundings and naturally cautious, Ricky gestured with a head nod in Divine's direction, then asked, *"Who di bwoy deh wit di yellow diamond pon him chest?"*

*"Mi never know him,"* said Sleepy, Ricky's head of security.

*"Don't bother yaself, father. We soon know him,"* said Smitty.

Being the man of his stature, he sent two bottles of Patrón to Divine when he saw him with a familiar face. This face happened to be Rah-Rah, his meanest bitch Tasha's little brother.

"Tasha, *dis mi brethren Divine from foreign,"* said Rah-Rah, introducing him.

She sized him up, then greeted him with a hug and a kiss to the right cheek, saying, *"Mi brother seh yuh him brother, so yuh mi brother."*

Watching this scene from afar, Ricky let his guard down because of the sign she gave him. Kissing him on the right cheek indicated that he was family, but a kiss to the left would've meant that he was fair game and to have the goons ready before the night was over. Making small talk, she asked him what brought him to the island, and he replied by telling her that he was looking for a reggae artist to sign to his label. She then asked what label he worked for, and he told her he was a partner in Hot Wax Records. Hearing this, her interest peaked because she was an avid listener of Sincere's music.

"I'm gonna bring you to Ricky because he has all the connections," she said, hoping that she'd get to meet Sincere one day for doing this small favor.

Over hearing this conversation, Cashmere said, "Hi! I'm Cashmere, and you are?"

Knowing her name from somewhere, he simplified his name by saying, "I'm D, and it's nice to meet you."

"What is it that you need help with?" she asked, trying to hypnotize him with her sex appeal.

"I'm looking for a reggae artist to sign to my record label," he said, ignoring the subtle flirting she did with her body language.

She was bad as fuck, so he cursed himself for being married. She was the girl that women didn't want crossing paths with their men because he would more than likely be subdued by her beauty.

"Oh, that's going to be simple because there's a lot of talent out here. Once Tasha sets up an appointment, you'll be good to go. Well, I have to be going. Enjoy your night," she said, as she strutted across the stage, making non-believers believe that a person could fall in love at first sight.

*** 

Curious about the guy with the yellow diamonds, both Smitty and Sleepy went on their separate missions to gather as much information as possible pertaining to him. Sleepy got in contact with a little breezy he was fucking, who worked at the airport, and she gave him the rundown on Divine, only because he promised to do what all Jamaicans denied doing — eat her pussy.

He was a pussy-eating mothafucka, and she loved it! She knew when he wasn't with her he would say, "*Bad mon nuh bow cat*," but she didn't care who he told that nonsense because she knew the real deal.

Smitty, on the other hand, had purchased a case of rum with intentions of making his spirit happy when it showed up to deliver the intelligence he was inquiring about Divine. He performed his ceremony, and his spirit came fast in search of rum. Possessing Smitty's body, the spirit said, "You have enough rum to make me happy, so you can have whatever you ask for."

After regaining control of his body, he popped in a tape from the sun splash to show the spirit Divine's image, but nothing prepared him for what was to come.

When the spirit saw the image, he reentered Smitty's body, then stood frozen, locked on Divine for a few seconds before throwing Smitty's helpless body into walls, door posts, and anything that couldn't be knocked over.

Breaking bottles of rum over Smitty's defenseless head, the spirit said, "This man is evil! Protected by evil! Born into evil and will die evil, so stay away from him!"

Leaving Smitty's body unscathed from the night's madness, the spirit rushed away as Smitty said, "All merciful, why do you run from the mention of this evil? You are most powerful."

Left without a response, Smitty was unsure of what to do next, so he went to sleep.

Rubies and Retribution

***

Out in Ocho Rios, at Ricky's villa, Divine was greeted by Tasha and Cashmere who both said,

*"Wah gwon, D? Cum in an' cool it."*

Sitting at an office desk that had to cost, at least, $20,000, Ricky sat draped in rubies! Ruby earrings, rings, bracelets, teeth, and a ruby encrusted skull medallion. Being in the presence of all those rubies, Divine caught an instant headache, but he blamed it on the oil Ricky wore.

*"Wah mi cyan do fi yuh, my yout? Mi hear yuh a DJ, who search fi bad mon tune. Dis true?"* said Ricky.

"Yes. I want the best artist Jamaica has to offer."

*"All right ... mi no mean yuh no disrespect when mi ask bout yuh age. Mi ask because mi swear pon mi mooma mi see dat lion head deh before."*

"I'm twenty-nine."

"*Hmm...*" Ricky paused, going over what Divine said before he said, "*Anyway, mi brother, when mi find wah yuh a look fah, we a link up. Yuh hear?*"

Ending their conversation, they reached over the table to give one another a handshake, but when they touched, they had the biggest shock known to man due to a buildup of static electricity.

Thinking nothing of it, they laughed it off, saying to one another the shock meant they were going to make a lot of money together, but in actuality, the shock was their two spirits at war.

As Divine exited the office, leaving Ricky alone, he walked by Smitty, who looked as if he'd just seen the devil himself. Thinking nothing of it, he said, "Have a good one."

Smitty watched Divine turn the corner. Then, he rushed into Ricky's office where he was surprised to see him twisting up a big head spliff.

"*Wah happen to yuh, mon?*" asked Ricky, annoyed because he had barged in unannounced.

"*Dat bwoy deh di devil ... yuh cyant trust him, Ricky!*" he replied.

Jokingly, Ricky said, "*Bumba clot! Obiah mek Smitty gone mad.*"

Laughing along with Ricky, his stomach knotted up and his mouth went dry, thinking to himself that it was impossible for his spirit to be afraid of something, so this mustn't be taken lightly. In order to alleviate the stress, he took a few pulls on Ricky's spliff, then convinced himself that he misunderstood what his spirit was trying to say.

*** 

Deep in thought, Divine went over all the day's events, knowing he was getting close to finding out what he was feeling was more than just that. He was on a mission, but he didn't want to dwell on the issue at hand, so he drank rum punch chased by Red Stripe throughout the night, pausing only to call Tessa, who he missed deeply, but the home phone rang and rang only to reach an answering machine.

Knowing she was still mad at him, he quit after the fifth attempt, justifying her anger with him because it was perfectly acceptable for her to be upset. He agreed with her, but the less she knew the better. Lying on his back with heavy eyelids, he pondered his next move, but he had no clue about what it would be if his theory proved to be right.

After falling asleep, his dreams were clear and flooded with the detail that the dreams of the past always lacked. In his reveries, he saw a man's face hiding behind a ski mask, laughing at him, revealing a set of gold teeth flooded with rubies. His second dream showed Robbery Rob and K-Blizz being shot in their legs and their heads by a curvy assailant with long hair. He didn't see a face, but he knew the silhouette of a woman when he saw one. Waking with a smile tattoed to his face, he called Playboy to tell him to be around when he came back from Jamaica. Hanging up the phone, he said, "This can't be right, but I don't believe in coincidences, so something's gotta give."

***

Deep in sleep, Smitty tossed and turned from horrible visions of people being decapitated, people being placed in tires, then set ablaze as they were rolled down hills and a world of other things. But what made him jump out of his bed was the image of snakes everywhere. The snakes were slithering through the eye sockets of skulls, in the mouths and out of the noses, but what scared him the most was the image of Divine's body completely made of snakes.

His ribs were made up of red and black pythons, his legs were made of green and black anacondas, his arms were made of tan copper heads, his feet and hands were a mixture of vipers, rattlers, and cobras all attached to the head and face of a man who sang a song he couldn't understand:

> "*Dambala se lwa koulev la ooooo.*
>
> *Dambala se lwa koulev la bali siro.*
>
> *Pou swiv yape pou swiv mwen la'a.*
>
> *Ala yape pou swiv ooooo.*
>
> *Se mwen min'm Ayida Wedooooo.*
>
> *Se mwen min'm Dambala Wedoooo.*
>
> *Yo poko we kote'm tounin koulev ooooo.*"

After seeing what he would call anarchy, he jumped out of his sleep more frightened than ever before, so he did something he hadn't done since he was a child — drop down on his knees to pray and ask the Lord Jesus Christ for forgiveness.

Rubies and Retribution

***

"Hey, Rah-Rah! I'm gone in a few days, so I want to flick it up for my first memories of Jamaica," said Divine.

"*Cool, my yout. Mi a call di Pum-Pum crew an dem a mek di pictures wicked!*"

"That's what I'm talking about, Rah. After the pictures, I just might bounce early 'cause I need to patch things up with my wife."

"*Yuh affi do wah yuh affi do so mi cyant vex.*"

After taking pictures of beautiful waterfalls, sunsets, celebrities, and, last but not least, the Pum-Pum crew, he headed home with his camera in tow.

***

"*Ricky, yuh cyant do business wit di bwoy from foreign!*" said Smitty, trying to give Ricky a heads up.

"*Smitty, yuh start mek mi vex! Long time mi wan yuh stop deal wit obiah but yuh nah listen an' now yuh gone mad!*"

"*Mad? Ricky last night mi do something mi nah do since mi a lickle pitny. Mi rise up an' get down on mi hand an' knee an' beg Jesus Christ fah fahgiveness.*"

"Hmmm," said Ricky, pondering about what was said.

"*Di bwoy wicked!*"

"*Him a DJ so cool it.*"

"*Mi nah seh him a try an' disrespect yuh, my lawd, but mi seh him a bad mon!*"

"*All right, mi a tink 'bout it,*" said Ricky, knowing he wasn't going to give Smitty's antics any serious thought.

\*\*\*

"What's good, my nigga?" asked Playboy, as he greeted Divine at the airport.

"I'm good, but we need to go down memory lane," said Divine.

"Why? What's good?"

"What does the word or name 'Cashmere' do for you?" asked Divine.

"Nothin' … matter of fact, Blizz had a bad bitch, a Dominican thang by that name."

"Come on. Let's get rid of this luggage. Then I'll put you on to what's on my mind."

Driving to Divine's house, Playboy listened to what Divine thought about Jamaica and the tie to his father's, Rob's, and Blizz's deaths.

"Get the fuck outta here!" shouted Playboy, as he sat in Divine's driveway, wanting to believe what he was hearing.

It was too far-fetched, and it was written all over his face, so Divine asked, "Do you remember when I told you I started to have nightmares shortly after I met Tessa? You know, when I came home from doing those four calendars for that drug beef."

"Yeah, I remember, but what that gotta do with what ya telling me?"

"I never told you or anybody else this, but my father's last words were to 'never forget the yardy with the rubies.' I was four years old, so I ain't know what the fuck he was talkin' 'bout, but now I understand."

"Understand what?"

"When I went to Haiti, I met my grandfather for the first time, and we did a lot of talkin', and the shit he said left me thinkin'."

"Talkin' and thinkin' 'bout what?"

"To sum everythin' up, he said rubies affect me in a strange way, so I shouldn't be around them when I lay my head down to rest. He's known for years who killed my father, but he didn't intervene 'cause this has to be my retribution. The icin' on the cake is that, when I find out who killed my pops, I'll find who killed Rob and Blizz."

"Okay?" he said, with an expression that said "I don't get it."

"What I'm tryin' to say is that Tessa wears ruby earrings she got from her father. Whenever she wears them, I have nightmares, but I didn't think nothin' of it until a few days after my return from Haiti. Since I been back, I told her not to wear them, and I been nightmare free up until the other day. I was sitting around, and my conversation with my grandfather popped up, so I had her wear them, and just like that, my nightmares came back. They came back strong, so one day I figured I had to go to Jamaica to find the yardy with the rubies. I found him all right! The mothafucka runs the whole island, so he can't be touched. Do you know what the craziest part is?"

"What's that?"

"This mothafucka looks just like Tessa!"

"Nah! Don't say that!"

"Real talk … the reason I think he's her father is because she always said her father loves rubies."

"Did he have any rubies on him?"

"Did he? He had on so many rubies that I got an instant headache when I was in his office."

"That's that nigga, son!"

"What also makes me believe that it's him is the fact that he swore he'd seen my lion head medallion before."

"He probably did. What's your point?"

"My father had this chain on the night he got killed."

"Oh, shit!"

"To top it off, my dreams became crystal clear after havin' the meetin' with him. Before the meetin', all my dreams were vague, but later that night, I dreamt of a man in a ski mask laughin', exposin' gold grills flooded with rubies. Normally, when I dreamt of Rob and Blizz, I saw them gettin' domed by an unknown person, but on that night, I saw a woman's silhouette from behind as she committed the act. For that reason, I took a bunch of pictures in every imaginable angle of the Pum-Pum crew, so now let's go inside to see these pictures when I upload them into the computer."

"Pum-Pum crew! What the fuck is that?"

"That's a team of the baddest bitches on earth whose sole purpose is to lure in any nigga or chick with money to get robbed and killed."

No one was home when they entered the mansion, so they went straight to the east wing's studio. Once there, Divine uploaded the pictures, and Playboy said, "Damn! Them bitches bad! What the fuck! I see why niggas be gettin' caught up."

Looking at a picture of Cashmere, Playboy thought long and hard about where it was he knew her from, then asked, "Who that?"

"I don't know," replied Divine, as he played stupid. "I know her, though. She sucked me off before. That's Blizz's pussy," said Playboy.

"You got sucked off, but you don't know her name?"

"I get sucked off by too many bitches to remember their names. It's hard to remember their names and even harder when you got a nigga like Blizz on the team. I fucked fourteen bitches in one week fuckin' with him."

"Damn! I been missing out since I got married, huh?"

"Hell yeah! We used to call you tender dick because you used to always be with Tessa back in the day."

"Tender dick? Yeah. A'ight. Y'all stupid for thinkin' that bullshit."

"Her name is Silky, Cotton, Denim, or some type of fabric. She used to set niggas up for Blizz."

Listening to Playboy, he sat anxiously waiting for her name to escape his boy's mouth, and that's when he shouted, "Cashmere … damn! We were just talking 'bout her. Do you think smokin' fucked up my memory?"

Happy that he spewed her name, Divine ignored his question, then said, "That's her, and she's the boss's wife. You said that she used to set niggas up for Blizz, right?"

"Yeah, he and Rob were usin' her to get Cubans, Columbians, and Dominicans with cash because she was bad and spoke Spanish."

"That nigga Blizz kept a bitch that did whatever he wanted," said Divine, shaking his head with a smile on his face.

"She was the only bitch he fucked with that wasn't at the funeral, but I ain't think nothin' of it back then."

"You right. I would've remembered her. My grandfather said, when I find one, I'll find the other, and I think that's what just happened."

"I feel you in regards to this nigga killin' ya pops, but how you gonna prove it's her who got our brothers?"

"I don't know," he said, as he went to take a swig of his Guinness.

As his eyes scanned over the pictures, the Guinness fell from his hand, staining his carpet. What provoked this action was a picture of Cashmere that looked identical to the silhouette in his dream. He shouted, "Oh, shit!"

"That's right," said Playboy, looking at his all white Harlems (uptowns) that were now stained with spilled Guinness.

"That's the silhouette from my dream! That's Cashmere! That bitch killed our brothers!" shouted Divine.

"Are you sure?"

"Sure as money spends."

"I don't know, but how we gonna get them if he runs the whole damn island?"

"Be easy. I got this, but it's gonna take some time."

\*\*\*

Unaware of Divine's return, Tessa was still steaming hot about his going to Jamaica, even after he knew she was against the whole idea. She knew she was jumping the gun when she reacted the way she did, but she had to act up a little bit to keep the relationship healthy. That was her little secret.

She knew he loved her, but being x-amount of miles away on a tropical island flooded with women and the notorious Pum-Pum crew wasn't a good situation for a married man. Hedonism alone was enough to make a man give in to temptation, so she felt a tad bit insecure.

Her mind was on hyper drive, so she didn't notice Playboy's Lexus in the driveway when she pulled up to the house. Preoccupied with her thoughts, she got the girls out of the car, then entered the main foyer of their home. Startled by her husband and Playboy's presence, she forgot about the anger she had pent up as she ran to him and jumped in his arms, hugging and kissing him.

"Baby, you're home!" she shouted.

"Daddy's home!" shouted both Trinity and Divinity.

"Dad, what's good?" asked B-G.

"Hi, girls! I missed y'all. It's good to be home," he said.

"Uncle Play-Play!" shouted Divinity, as she ran to give him a big hug.

"Hi, uncle," said Trinity.

"Playa-Playa, what's good?" asked B-G.

"How's my little nieces?" he asked, as he gave them a great, big group bear hug.

"Baby, I'm not mad at you," said Tessa.

"Yes, you are 'cause you ain't answer my calls. It's cool, though. We'll talk about it later."

"Okay. I'm holding you to that Divine, or else," she said, balling up her little fists and positioning herself like the Fighting Irish guy from Notre Dame.

"Even though I was there for business, I enjoyed myself, and I can't wait to go with you guys next year. The weather was a small piece of heaven. Now let's get comfortable, so I can tell you what took place out there."

# Chapter 6

# One Year Later

*"Tessie bear, it's good to see yuh. Weh di girls deh?"* asked Ricardo, greeting his only daughter.

"They're with their father."

"*Mi tired a di bwoy fuckery!*"

"Cool it, Dad … they're at the hotel unpacking."

"Oh! Mi tink him keep dem a foreign."

"No. He was anxious to come, and he'll be here shortly."

"All right. Now mi affi teach him 'bout yard."

Shortly after her conversation with her father, she was greeted by Divine and their three little girls, who were more than adorable.

"Grandpa Ricardo!" shouted Trinity and Divinity, as they raced toward him.

"*Wah gwon, Gramps?*" asked B-G with her best Jamaican patois.

"*Hey, yu … lickle gangsta … cum,*" said Ricardo, as he picked her up, placing her onto his shoulder.

Coming from behind Ricardo, Divine's stomach was in knots because he knew the man who murdered his dad was his wife's father. He was yet to have the solid proof to act on what he felt up until the moment because Ricardo turned around, smiling at B-G's attempt at patois.

*"Bumba clot! DJ, a yu mi daughter husband?"* he asked, realizing he already knew Divine.

Giving Divine a big hug, he found a new love for him because his daughter always spoke highly of him.

"Ricky!" he shouted, trying his best to seem surprised while facing a dilemma. He was happy to prove his theory correct but upset that Tessa, the love of his life, was going to suffer in order for him to receive his retribution.

Tessa's curiosity peaked, so she looked back and forth between the two of them, then asked, "Am I missing something? How do you two know each other?"

*"Dis a di DJ mi tell yuh cum from foreign a look fah bad mon tune,"* said Ricardo.

She knew he wasn't cheating but hearing it aloud didn't hurt one bit.

"So did you guys hit it off when you met? How did you meet? I know the island is small, but it's not that small," she asked, extremely curious.

"I linked up with my man Rah-Rah, who has a sister that is a friend of your father's at the Reggae Sun Splash."

Accepting the explanation, they moved on, surrounded by a small army as an escort to a private beach, where they would enjoy the beautiful waters of Jamaica.

Once on the beach, Ricky's staff of waiters prepared rum-punch and mimosas for the adults and an assortment of fruit juices for the girls.

There was corn, red snapper, and conch being grilled to perfection by a chef that loved his cooking so much he boasted, saying, *"Yuh neva yom food dis good back a foreign."*

Entertainment was provided by an upcoming band while Tessa and Divine cuddled like two lovebirds. The mood was right, and she felt completely comfortable in his arms, so she said,

"I love you more than life itself, Mr. Jean-Baptiste."

"I love you more, Mrs. Jean-Baptiste," he said, as he took her by the hand, so they could take a romantic walk while the sun set.

Coming to the shore line of the white sand beach, she was giddy like a school girl with a crush, so she said, "Look out there, Divine. Do you see the little island out there?"

"Where? I don't see it."

"Out there," she said, pointing in the direction of the deep blue sea.

Easing up from behind, he wrapped his arms around her, then followed the direction of her finger until he finally saw the little island she spoke of.

"I see it now, bae."

She was the adventurous type, so she said, "Good. I'll meet you there," right before she took a mad dash into the warm waters.

"Damn! This girl always got me doin' shit I got no business doin'," he said, as he followed suit.

Splashing through the waters, she taunted him, saying, "If you can't keep up with me in the water, how will you keep up with me in the bed?"

Ignoring her comment, he swam at a steady pace which brought him to the shores of the little island slightly ahead of her. Sprawled out on the white sand, short of breath, he waited on her to arrive, and when she did, she looked marvelous! Her caramel skin glistened in the sun as her toned legs and pedicured toes parted the sand. Her nipples were erect, poking through her bikini top, giving him a tingle in his loins, making his mouth water.

The look of desire was in his eyes as she walked toward him, so she straddled him, then gave him a long, passionate kiss. Lost in her soft lips, he squeezed her big ole ass.

While their lips pressed firmly against each other, she felt him begin to rise to the occasion, so she said, "Slow down, soldier. We have a whole island to explore." Then, she jumped off him and headed into the forest.

Following closely behind, he had a crazy hard-on from watching her booty jiggle with every step. All her succulent flesh bounced, driving him mad due to it being completely exposed by the g-string she wore. Hypnotized by her curves, he didn't notice when she came to a stop, so he bumped into her, poking her with his blood-filled tool, making her say, "If you weren't watching my booty, you would've noticed that I stopped."

"I can't help it! That thang fat as fuck!" he said, as he smacked her fatty.

"Boy, take your eyes off my ass, so you can see what it is that made me stop."

"What you see?"

"Do you see that cave over there?"

"Yeah, I see it, but we ain't goin' in there, Tessa."

"Why not?"

"If you don't know, let's just say 'cause we don't know what's in that mothafucka!"

"You're no fun," she said, heading toward the entrance of the cave.

"Tessa, stop playin'! If somethin' happens to you, how I'm goin' to tell the girls and your father?"

Ignoring him, she continued toward the cave, saying, "Come on!"

While following her into the cave reluctantly, he thought, women are always a man's downfall, dating back to when Eve got Adam jammed up with the Lord.

Upon entry into the cave, it felt cool due to a breeze that indicated there was an opening somewhere on the other side. Following the path from which the breeze originated, they heard a faint sound of running water that grew louder with their every step. The closer they got to the origins of this water, the more the faint trickle they had heard turned into a roaring waterfall, so intrigue was an understatement. When they finally made it to the opening, they were engulfed with a mist from splashing water that cascaded off rocks at the base of the mountain. This opening was behind a waterfall that dropped hundreds of feet, pouring millions of gallons into the canyon.

To the left of the waterfall, one could see yellow and green vegetation. To the right, one could take a glimpse of the entire island in its natural beauty. The view was magnificent, so they stood there in awe, at a loss for words, until Tessa said, "Make love to me right here, Divine. This is such a perfect place."

Silently taking his orders, he removed her bikini top while placing kisses on her collarbone. Their bodies were wet from the spraying mist of the waterfall, so their hands slid gracefully over one another as they caressed. She was anxious to baptize this cave, so she removed his swimming trunks, revealing a swollen penis. His shaft dripped pre-cum, so she said, "Isn't somebody happy to see me?"

"Always is and you know that," he said, as he pulled her g-string down low enough for her to step out of it.

Rubbing two fingers over her fold he saw that she was soaked, so he let the games begin. Seeing how excited she was, he bowed down to one knee, placing her right leg over his shoulder, so he could taste her love. He licked slowly but steadily for a while because that was how she liked it. He licked her clit with the pattern of S over and over as she thrust her hips forward, leaving pussy juice all over his face.

Nearing her climax, she gyrated her hips faster and faster while rubbing his bald head, saying, "Right there, daddy. Don't stop. That's my spot."

He loved pleasing his woman as every man should, so he went hard until she begged for him to stop. His tonguin' was too good, so she pushed his head away from her coochy, saying,

"Stop please. Stop. I can't take no more!"

Removing her leg from his shoulder, she sat him down on a smooth rock. Taking in a mouth and throat full of her baby, she went to work at pleasing him by bobbing up and down, while gently caressing his testicles. She licked the sides of his shaft and sucked on his balls until he moaned in delight. She enjoyed pleasing her man as every woman should, so she went hard, stopping only to suck his nipples and say, "Cum for me, daddy."

He was in ecstasy! Her saliva dripped from his cock while she did her thing, and he ran his fingers through her hair with one hand while playing with her clit with the other. His fingers were talented, so she moaned from his touch while she made his toes curl from the exceptional job she was doing. She was doing such an outstanding job, he said, "Suck that dick! Got damn, Tessa. You the best!"

Pleased by pleasing him, she felt he was about to cum because he jumped and tightened up in her mouth. This indication made her switch positions to allow him room to stand while she continued doing her thing. She now grabbed his ass, then pushed and pulled him to and fro, so he could fuck her face until he came. Now stroking her mouth without guidance, he let out a mother load that filled her throat and stomach. After swallowing his children, she continued to go in to assure that he didn't go soft, so they could get to bumping and grinding. She succeeded at her task of keeping him aroused because the smacking of her lips with the cock and deep throating kept him as hard as the beams holding up the Golden Gate Bridge in San Francisco.

Eager to feel him move around inside of her stomach, she straddled him, then gently rubbed the head of his eight-inch against her love to coat it with juices. The rubbing of his penis against her clit back and forth for a while was enough to drive them both crazy but enough was enough, so she inserted his pipe to the depths of her belly. Sitting still on his lap with him all the way inside, she rolled her hips, grinding her clitoris into his pelvic bone for maximum stimulation. She kissed and licked his bald head while he spread and squeezed her butt cheeks. He pulled her into him while thrusting upward, aiming for all the right places, and she enjoyed every minute of it.

They went at each other in the confines of the cave for a while, making each other cum and cum again. For their final round, he had her switch positions from front to back and side to side all the way up until he felt his climax nearing. Feeling the tingling sensation, he laid on his back, then motioned for her to get on top, but in the reverse cowgirl position, so her back was facing him, awarding him the opportunity to watch her pop that booty up and down on his shaft.

She loved being on top because it gave her full control. It was something he didn't mind giving up every now and then because she made it do what it do. As she worked her love muscle over his shaft, he said, "Damn, baby ... put that pussy on me!"

"You like that?" she asked, sweating from her workout.

"Hell, yeah! Don't stop!"

"Boy, you feel good! This is my dick, so know that, if you give it away, I'll kill you," she said, while climaxing.

Anxious to make him blow, she came up to the head of his manhood, then popped that pussy up and down, making him stumble over his words, "Oh! Sh-shit!"

"Damn."

"Shit."

"G."

"Get."

"Get off me."

"I'm about to bust!"

She had it going on in the bedroom, so she knew there wasn't any fronting on his behalf while he stumbled over his words. He was a watcher. He loved watching his pipe slide in and out of a wet pussy, and for that fact, he was in heaven because her oils had his pipe glossy as she slid up and down. His toes were curling because he was nearing his climax, and she knew it, so she squeezed her walls around him to help him release. Feeling a surge of hot semen rising from his loins, he said, "I'm cummin'!"

"I got it, baby," she said, as she jumped off him in order to deep throat him until she caught every drop. She caught every drop and swallowed, so he got another hard-on because it was such a turn on to see his baby in her freak mode.

He thought, every man wants a lady in the streets, but to keep him happy at home, she has to be a freak in the bed. Fortunate enough to have both, he said, "Damn! I love you, you nasty bitch!" with a smile on his face.

Holding his pipe in her hand with a smile as cum rested on her chin, she said, "You better."

\*\*\*

Spending time alone with his granddaughter, Ricardo said to B-G, "*Yuh stay like yuh thuggy thuggy. Wah gwon?*"

"I'm a G, Grandpa," she replied.

Looking at his precious grand baby with a smile on his face, he said, "*Yuh affi slow down an enjoy yuh yout,*" as she tried her hand at climbing a tree in search of coconuts.

To the left of them, Divinity was building a sand castle for her black Barbie doll, having so much fun, she was oblivious to the hermit crab walking alongside the gates of her castle. If she would've seen it, her overactive imagination would've made her believe the crab was a team of invaders trying to kidnap her black Barbie princess.

Trinity was to the right of them, sipping pineapple juice, getting a tan, reading a Berenstein Bears book and loving the tropical weather and the tranquil atmosphere, so she said, "I want to move to Jamaica."

"*Yuh cyan, Trini, but not now cuz yuh still a pitny,*" said Ricardo.

"Grandpa, I'm grown," she said, as she rolled her eyes in between sips of pineapple juice.

"Grandpa, I'm hungry," said Divinity.

"Me, too, Gramps," said B-G.

"*All right, yuh affi full yuh belly wit good cookin'*," he said, as they headed toward an immaculately handcrafted table designed by a local carpenter.

Once seated, they were served fruit cocktails consisting of mango, cantaloupe, strawberry, and pineapple as an appetizer. Enjoying the company of his beloved grandchildren, he basked in the moment all while he enjoyed a beautiful sunset.

"Awww! That's pretty," said Trinity, as she pointed to the sunset.

"Can I have one, Grandpa?" asked Divinity, pointing to the sky.

"*Blood clot! Dem de tings deh yuh cyant buy, Diviny.*"

"That's what's up," said B-G, as she stared at the orange and yellow hues of the sunset, resting above the blue ocean.

Joining them at the table for what seemed to be a feast fit for kings, Tessa said, "Dad, this is beautiful," complimenting the art and patience needed to make this gourmet cuisine.

*"Dis yah a notin, dumplin'. Dis a everyday ting."*

Enjoying the Caribbean climate and spices in the food, Divine said, "It's good to have finally made it here with the family, Ricardo."

*"Mi happy yuh cum ... call mi Ricky."*

"I haven't heard from you, so it's safe to say you haven't heard anyone or any group that would peak my interest with their music."

*"Easy no, mon ... Dis a Ricky yuh par wit ... Once mi hear mi daughter man a di DJ mi find a wicked tune an' him affi com perform fi yu."*

And as if on cue, Divine heard drums, organs, guitars, and maracas sound off simultaneously, making B-

G lick shots with her mouth while pointing two fingers in the air, "Boop! Boop! Boop!"

Everyone laughed at her antics, but they all fell silent when the artist sang the lyrics to an original song he wrote. The words were captivating! He had everyone in a trance because the song was both hard and political.

After wrapping up a three-song show, he was introduced to Divine by Ricky who loved what he'd heard, so he was on the phone with both Mizzle and Maniac Main, telling them to get in the lab because they needed some hard reggae beats.

"I like what you did tonight, so I want to sign you to Hot Wax Records."

"*Yuh cyant be serious*," said the artist.

"*Really an' truly ... Di boss yah genuine, mi brother*," said Ricky to the artist.

"*Bumba clot! Give thanks, yuh hear?*" said the artist.

"We're gonna make each other a lot of money, so don't stop makin' those hits ... my lawyer will be contacting you sometime next week, so be prepared to get into the studio."

"*Cool! Mi ready long time!*" said the artist, as he departed for the night, anxious to tell his family the good news.

"*Yuh like wha yuh hear?*"

"Hell, yeah! What do I owe you for this?" asked Divine.

"*Neva mind yahself. All yuh affi do is tek care of mi dumpling, yuh hear? Cyan yuh handle it?*"

"Yes! That's the love of my life."

"*Yuh better cuz we a war if anyting happen to mi daughter.*"

Making no response to his comment, Divine thought, If you knew I was taking you to war as we speak, you wouldn't be so cocky, threatening me.

Lil Haiti

\*\*\*

"*Yo, shotta yout! Mi have a ting fi yuh,*" said Divine to a young boy who looked like he was down for whatever.

"*Wah gwon, big mon?*" he asked.

"*Mi have a lickle ting fi yuh deal wit,*" said Divine, knowing that the young boy was hungry and down for whatever. Murder could be read from his eyes.

"*Wah dat, boss?*"

"*Yuh move like yuh a shotta, so mi have ten grand US fi yuh mek a duppy.*"

"*Ten Gs! Weh him deh?*" asked the young boy, anxious to slump something for ten grand.

"*Cool it, no mon. Yuh nah promise to mek it back because di bwoy have money an' pure shotta wit him,*" he said, giving the young boy a warning.

"*Who yuh a chat 'bout? Neva mind yahself, mi brother. Di pussy ole Ricky yu a talk.*"

"*Hmmm. Mi have di machine dem, ten G US dollar, an a separate twenty G fi yuh family if yuh nah mek it back,*" said Divine, sweetening the pot.

"*Mi wan di pussy hole dead long time! Him kill off all mi brother dem,*" shouted the young boy.

"*Tek dis five G fi shot an vest.*"

"Cool," said the young boy, knowing that he wasn't going to spend anywhere close to five stacks on bullets and vests.

"*Yuh have di money when everyting crisp,*" said Divine, as he departed.

\*\*\*

"Dad, how do you like Divine?" asked Tessa.

*"Who di DJ? Mi like him because him seem cool, but mi neva understand why him familiar in him face."*

"He's good to me, Dad. He takes care of us financially, and he's there both physically and emotionally. He loves us unconditionally, so he'll put his life on the line to keep us safe."

*"Dat mi like! A mon who love him family a dangerous mon, member mi tell yuh."*

"It feels good to be around you, Dad."

*"Mi know ... all di gyal tell mi so,"* he said, laughing at his own joke.

"You're so nasty!"

*"Nasty! Gyal yuh mad! A yuh di lickle sketal who run off wit' her man tree day ago."*

Guilty as sin, she couldn't do anything but blush, knowing that her father knew what went on when she and her husband disappeared the other day.

*"Why yuh get quiet? Gyal, yuh have tree pitny, so mi know yuh tek wood in a yuh belly."*

"Dad!" she exclaimed, embarrassed as he spoke about her in such a manner.

The night was coming to a close as they sat on the patio, reminiscing about her childhood.

They drank Bailey's until two in the morning, until they were tipsy. Dozing off with her head on her father's shoulder, she thought to herself that life was good because she was financially stable and happy emotionally, spiritually, and sexually. But what made her fall asleep with a smile on her face was the fact she had two very important men in her life. Her father was one, and her husband was the other.

\*\*\*

Lurking in the shadows, the young boy that Divine had put on the mission waited outside of one of Ricky's many clubs, eager to squeeze off on him. He knew Ricky would have an entourage of security with him, so he would have to move stealthily.

Stepping out of the club, tipsy off stone and white rum, Ricky said, *"Hey, Sleepy! Weh yuh deh? Mi wood rise up an mi wan Cashmere fi lick pon mi cocky."*

*"All right, boss. Mi a call."*

Oblivious to the young boy in the shadows, Ricardo proceeded to his military issued Hummer without a care in the world until his heart skipped a beat and his liquor high went out the window when he heard, Blocka! Blocka! Blocka! and *"Bumba clot!"* as shots rang out, hitting one of his security guards.

Rushing Ricky to the Humvee, Sleepy told the rest of the security detail to find the culprit, kill him, and leave the bones, but to bring the skin back to him. Knowing it would get ugly if Ricky's guards caught up to him, he took off into the darkness of Spanish Town, cursing himself for missing his intended target. The security searched high and low for the hit man underneath cars, in dumpsters, backyards, and the roofs of lowrise bungalows, but they ended up with nothing.

*** 

After two hours of searching the neighboring blocks, they returned to Ricky's mansion to give him the bad news.

"*Ricky, mi have bad news,*" said Skalla.

"*Wah type a fuckery yuh a chat?*" exclaimed Ricky, slamming his fist into his office table. "*Sum bwoy try an tek off mi head an yuh a chat 'bout bad news! Mi and mi alone bad news ... mi alone a kill off him whole blood clot family.*"

"*Cool it, Ricky. Hear wah him affi seh,*" said Sleepy.

"*We have double bad news. We cyant find him an' dem kill Juicy.*"

"*Wah di bumba?*" asked Ricky, looking to the heavens for an answer.

The office grew silent as everyone said a prayer for Juicy, but the silence was shattered when Smitty damn near broke the office door down, ranting, "*It a di DJ mon. Di DJ fiya shot pon yuh, Ricky.*"

Startling everyone with his outburst, he was restrained by security as Ricky said, "*Smitty gon mad. Tek him back a di house an shot him cuz him start mek mi vex.*"

"*Ricky, yuh mad! Yuh cyant kill Smitty,*" said Skalla, intervening.

"*Cool ... mi cool jus mek him gway from here so.*"

"*Don't bother yahself father mi handle it,*" said Sleepy.

*"All right ... gway from here ... mi affi tink."*

Sitting alone in the dark office, with Cashmere underneath the table sucking him off, Ricky thought about what Smitty said, so he called Tessa to ask for Divine's whereabouts.

"Hey, Dumplin."

"Hi, Dad! Are you okay? It's four in the morning."

*"Everyting crisp. Weh di DJ?"*

"He's right here, snoring loud enough to wake up the dead," she said, as she put the phone on speaker to give him a chance to hear for himself.

*"Sheesh! Mi see why yuh cyant sleep!"*

"I've been up on the computer for the last six hours, dealing with this walking-talking lawn mower."

"Ha! Ha!" He laughed at her humor.

"What's wrong, Dad?"

*"Nothin'. Mi a jus mek sure yuh crisp."*

"You sure, Dad?"

"*Yeah, don't bother yahself, Dumplin.*"

With a hesitant tone in her voice, she said, "All right, Dad … I love you."

"*Mi know … mi love you, too,*" he said, as he hung up the phone.

Convincing himself there wasn't anything too serious or worrisome in regard to Smitty's claim, he leaned back in his recliner, so he could enjoy Cashmere's head job.

\*\*\*

Mad that he'd failed his mission, the young boy paced back and forth in his room, contemplating his next attempt. Loading his Mac-11, he wondered if what he'd heard about Ricky's vehicles was true because the entire island was led to believe that his fleet of cars were bulletproof. No one had dared to find out whether this was folklore or fact up until now because he was planning on airing out any vehicle he thought Ricky occupied.

The following day, the young boy arose early with a heart full of murder and rage, so he headed out to commit his daily crimes. He was becoming blinded by vengeance and very impatient, so he decided to strike in broad daylight, after Ricky did exactly what he thought he would do. Keep routine.

Every day, Ricky went to a roti spot for lunch at one in the afternoon, but today was different because he was unaware of a young boy roaming the streets, armed with a fifty shot Mac-11 in pursuit of justice.

Today Ricky opted for a conch roti and drank a sorrel drink to give him the protein that he needed to last all night with Cashmere and whomever else he decided to bring into his bed. Stepping onto the curb with a stuffed belly, looking east and west, neither he nor his security spotted the young boy coming out of the alley with death in his eyes. The only thing that saved him and everybody else on the sidewalk was a children's school bus pulling up to say, "*Give thanks, Ricky. Yuh hear?*"

"*It a nothin',*" said Ricky, as he got in the backseat of his 750Li BMW.

He had a heart, so he couldn't spray the school bus; therefore, he waited for it to pull off, and when it did, he let shots fly like fireworks on the Fourth of July.

"Pa cong, cong, cong, cong, cong, cong, cong, cong, cong," rang out thirty times before he realized that what he'd heard about Ricky's cars was true.

On the inside of the car, everyone ducked, even though the whip was bulletproof. They weren't taking any chances because they'd heard loud shots and what sounded like a thousand pebbles hitting the hood of the Beamer.

Noticing that not even one shot had penetrated the vehicles exterior, the young boy got the fuck up out of there, hitting fences in every backyard.

After waiting a few seconds, after all shots ceased, they sat upright to see what was going on, but after surveying the scene, they saw nothing because the hit man was already gone.

"*Dis nah g' happen again*," said Ricky, through clenched teeth.

***

Sipping cosmopolitans, Cashmere and Tessa watched Divine ride the girls on a seadoo.

"You love him with all of your heart, Tessa?" asked Cashmere.

"Is it that obvious?"

"Yes, it is. It's written all over your face, and I envy you for that."

"What's there to envy? You're with my father, and he adores you."

"Ha, ha … your father adores any woman with a fat ass, honey. He's with a different woman every night."

"Why do you stick around?"

"Honestly. I don't know."

"If you're not happy, you'll have to go find your true love because you'll only be torturing yourself."

"I lost my true love many years ago, and I guess I'm living the cliché of 'if you can't have the one you love, love the one you're with.'"

"I'm sorry to hear about that. Do you mind telling me how, and what his name was?"

"His name was K-Blizz. Let's just say my greed for money got in between us and he died shortly after."

"Be strong and patient because love will come back around."

"I doubt it because I have a date with karma, and we all know she's a bitch."

"Ring, ring, ring," interrupted their conversation when Cashmere's phone went off.

Answering on the third ring, she could tell Ricky was troubled by something, so she asked, "What's wrong?"

And he shouted through the phone's receiver, *"Some pussy jus fiya shot pon mi an Smitty tink it a di DJ!"*

"It can't be because I've been with him, your daughter, and granddaughters all day."

"Oh, yeah?"

"Aren't you the one who said Smitty lost his mind? I know you did, so why do you believe him now?"

*"Mi neva know. Mi jus parrow."*

"We'll find whoever it is and put an end to this situation as soon as possible."

*"Respect, yuh hear?"* said Ricky, as he hung up.

"Is everything all right?" asked Tessa.

"Yes, nothing to worry yourself over. Somebody shot up your father's car."

"Oh, my God! Is he okay?"

"Yes, my dear. His cars are bulletproof, so no one was hurt."

"Are we in danger? If not, why was he asking about us?"

"I highly doubt you're in danger. He only asked about Divine because Smitty has been saying that he's the one responsible for the attempts on Ricky's life. Smitty has lost his mind, so disregard that."

"So that's why he asked me if Divine was with me the other night."

"Probably so."

Lost in their conversation, they didn't notice Divine sitting next to them, listening to their every word until he burst out, saying, "This fuckin' vacation is over! Tessa, pack your shit or get left!"

Then, he stormed off.

As he stormed off, he thought to himself that his plan was working and looked promising. Having completed the first phase of his plan, it was now time to take the next step.

*** 

"Ricky, do you think your daughter and family are safe?" asked Cashmere.

"*Dis yah nothin'. Dem bwoy know dat if dem touch mi pitny mi alone a bun di whole a Jamaica.*"

"They're packing because Divine is mad that you'd actually think he would try to harm you when harming you is harming Tessa."

"*All right! Mi understand him vex, but dat a good ting. Let dem go an mi a tell dem it's fi dem safety.*"

"Are you sure?"

"*Yeah, now gway from here, pretty gyal. Yuh mek mi wood rise up.*"

Smiling, due to his compliment, she thought about K-Blizz, her true love. Then her smile quickly faded and turned into a frown. Her heart was now full of pain, so she left Ricky's office feeling like shit.

***

"*Hey, Dumplin! Mi sorry dis fuckery a gwon an' mash up yuh vacation, but it better yuh back a foreign until tings die out over here so.*"

"I understand. And I want you to be careful and remember that I love you."

"*Mi a bad mon so everyting crisp.*"

"*Trini, Diviny, an Thuggy-Thuggy cum ... cum give Granddaddy a hug befah yuh tek off.*"

"I'm going to miss you, Grandpa," said both Trinity and Divinity, as they gave him a group hug.

*"Gramps, yuh be easy, yuh hear? 'Cause it nah do yuh no good if yuh mek mi vex,"* said B-G, surprising everybody with how clear her patois was.

*"Bumba cloooot!"* exclaimed Ricky, as he picked up B-G, hugging, kissing, and tickling her as he spun around in circles, overly joyed by his youngest granddaughter's display of patois.

Putting her down, he extended a hand to shake Divine's hand, but Divine looked him in the eye, then brushed by him as he boarded the plane.

\*\*\*

Deep in sleep, Smitty dreamed about women and money until one of their faces turned into that of a snake, then began to taunt, pick, and laugh at him. Tossing and turning, he had horrible visions throughout the night because he saw anacondas swallowing people whole. What petrified him the most was that the last person he saw being swallowed was himself.

Paralyzed in fear, he saw the image of Divine's head on an anaconda's body with a rattle snake's tail, laughing, while saying, "You're all going to die."

This horrible sight gave him a bad case of diarrhea, making him defecate all over himself for two hours straight until he defecated out his insides, organ by organ. His intestines came out as he yelled for help. His stomach lining came out in a pool of blood and muck that would remind one of the afterbirth of a woman's labor. Left to die alone in his bed, he cried silent tears as Alix, on the neighboring island of Haiti, thanked Dambala for eradicating his mystical enemy in Jamaica.

\*\*\*

Soaring above the clouds in Divine's company G5 jet, Tessa was upset because their vacation had ended early, but she completely understood how he felt. She knew how much it hurt to know that someone didn't trust you when you had taken a genuine liking to them, so she let him handle it alone until he was ready to talk.

She thought, It must be hard for him to love me the way he does, yet not be trusted by my father. So she tried to lighten the mood by saying, "Bae, I love you, and if you never want to see my father again, that's fine, but don't let a clouded mind allow you to forget that we have a genuine love for one another ... a love so real Cashmere envies us."

"Is that right? Somethin' 'bout her rubs me the wrong way."

"Yes, that's right. She poured her heart out to me while you were out on the water with the girls."

"I don't give a fuck 'bout her problems!"

"Well, you're going to hear about them anyway because she touched me."

He knew he was going to hear it, so he picked up a *Billboard* magazine in an attempt to ignore her. He read article after article until he heard her say Cashmere had lost her true love years ago, a guy by the name of K-Blizz. Startled by her words, he dropped the magazine, then asked, "What you just say?"

"What? Were you not listening to what I was saying? That's what I hate about you, Divine! You're bull-headed."

"Never mind that shit you talkin' 'bout. What you say his name was?"

"I said his name was K-Blizz."

"Did she say how he died?"

"What she said was rather vague, indicating that there was more to the story."

Losing his patience, he wanted to go upside her head for beating around the bush, but he remained calm because he didn't want to reveal that he had a lot of interest in Cashmere.

"What exactly did she say? Give me a quote."

"She said his name was K-Blizz, and 'let's say my greed for money got in between us and he died shortly after' ... I told her to be strong and patient because love will come back around to her, and then she said she doubted it because she has an upcoming date with karma."

"Is that right?" he asked, while the wheels in his head turned, giving him an idea of how to kill her now that the proof was in the pudding.

"I think she cheated with someone who was ballin', and in the process of creeping on him, he was killed."

Without giving any thought to her last words, he knew that grimy bitch Cashmere had killed his brothers, so his wrath was going to be felt.

\*\*\*

While Divine and his family were soaring over the Atlantic Ocean, the young boy was back in Jamaica, calculating the moves for his next attempt on Ricky's life. He knew from doing surveillance that Ricky got his dreads washed, conditioned, and spun down to the roots on the third week of every month, so he would be there to greet him with his Phoenix Arms .40 cal.

He wanted this mission to be over, but he didn't want to die in the process. This fact was the only reason Ricky was still alive.

Driving a stolen Honda Civic, he parked two blocks away, then walked to the salon. Upon his arrival, nothing prepared him for the beauty of Cashmere, who gave Ricky a hug before crossing the street to enter a pharmacy. He watched her hips sway side to side and back and forth, similar to a flag on a windy day. The remarkable view aroused him momentarily, making him forget about the mission at hand. After regaining his composure, he spotted Ricky entering the salon, so he decided to go into a local candy store, which carried children's smoke bombs, firecrackers, and things of that nature. He bought five smoke bombs, a pack of firecrackers, some yarn, and lighter fluid while there, so he could execute his plan. He knew security would be extra tight since he'd already made two unsuccessful attempts on Ricky's life; therefore, precautionary measures were necessary.

Ricky's treatment usually took two hours, so the young boy had time to burn, granting him free time to see if he could get some rhythm from the pretty thing he saw Ricky with a little while ago. After soaking the yarn with lighter fluid, he then tied it to the wick of the firecrackers, so he could detonate the pack from the opposite side of the block. Dropping the firecrackers at the intersection of the east side of the block, he walked by the salon, stretching the yarn out with him every step of the way until he reached an alley before the intersection of the west side.

After discreetly placing the yarn down, he went in pursuit of Cashmere in the pharmacy, where he spotted her in the cosmetic aisle getting Dove, Oil of Olay, and Camay soaps.

She was perfection at its best, so he said, "I see why your skin looks so smooth and soft ... it's because you use the right soaps. Let me guess, you use Palmer's Cocoa Butter for lotion, huh?"

Smiling, she said, "You must be the Peeping Tom I chased away from my bedroom window."

Laughing at her comment, he said, "I'm K-B, and you are?"

"I'm Cashmere, and it's nice to meet you, K-B."

"Likewise. I don't want to seem blunt, but I like what I see, and I'd like to take you out some time, so we could get to know each other better. Would that be possible?" he said, trying to cut to the chase.

"That sounds like an idea, so let me take your number," she said, reaching for her phone to store his number in the memory bank.

"Here we go ... this is a two-way conversation, pretty lady, so two numbers should be exchanged," said K-B, thinking she was going to take his number but never use it.

"Listen, honey. Don't mess up the opportunity I'm giving you. First thing against you is your age, but I'm able to look past that, so don't come on too strong because it's easier for me to not deal with you than it is to deal with you. Trust me. I'll call you."

"All right, you seem like a woman of her word," he said, as he gave her his cell phone number.

As she was punching his number into her phone, he noticed Sleepy, the head of Ricky's security detail, step outside the salon to do a quick scan of the area. This was to ensure his safety. He wouldn't allow Ricky to come outside if the scene wasn't deemed safe.

Knowing this, the young boy said, "Oh, shit, gorgeous! Did you get that number?"

"Yes, why? What's wrong?"

"I just saw a tow truck drive by, and my car is running and double-parked, so I have to run."

"Okay. I'll call you when I have some free time," she said, taking a genuine liking to his young ass.

Rushing out the pharmacy, he walked swiftly to the intersection on the west side of the block, then ducked into the alley where he'd left the yarn earlier.

Peeking around the corner, waiting for Ricky to step outside, he flicked the lighter on and off until he saw Sleepy step back out. Seeing Sleepy indicated that his target was on his way out, so he lit the yarn which acted as an extended wick for the firecrackers. The yarn burned right below Sleepy, undetected, so he motioned for Ricky to come outside. Seeing the signal Sleepy sent, he lit the five smoke bombs, then tossed them under Ricky's parked car. Stepping out of the salon, Ricky felt good, not caring that true Rastas called him a fashion dread since he got his done monthly. His only concerns were getting money and looking good, so he wasn't sweating any Rastafarians. Lost in his thoughts, he came back to reality when he noticed smoke coming from under his Beamer. The smoke made him say, "*Wah di blood clot! Di cyar pon fiya so mi affi,*" but his speech was cut short mid-sentence because he heard, "Pop, pop, pop, pop, pop, pop."

Dropping low to the ground, Ricky and his security were blinded by smoke, and that was when K-B made his move. Darting at his mark, insane with vengeance, he squeezed off two shots. Blocka! Blocka! He hit Sleepy in the stomach with one shot and Ricky in the neck with the other.

Screaming in agony, both Ricky and Sleepy were flanked by security that fired shots blindly in K-B's direction. Watching all the mayhem from the doorstep of the pharmacy, Cashmere jumped into attack mode, pulling out her .380 caliber semi-automatic Browning pistol. She approached K-B from behind, placing the cold steel on his neck, and he froze. She disarmed him as the smoke cleared, saying, "I told you, don't mess up.'"

"Damn, gorgeous! I thought you were a good girl," he said, knowing he was a dead man.

"No, honey. I'm a bad bitch!" she said, as she put two shots into his neck.

Rushing to Ricky's personal doctor, Cashmere broke every traffic law known to man. Once there, the doctor treated the both of them, then gave them strict orders to stay in bed and rest for a month.

Arriving at his mansion wounded, Ricky shouted orders for his people to find out if this was a man out for vengeance or if he was working with a team that planned on continuing these attacks.

Two hours after barking his orders, Johnny brought a sheet of paper to Ricky that displayed a picture of K-B and a list of his next of kin, living and deceased. Reading the names of K-B's kin, he could remember their faces as the life drained from their bodies when he murdered them, so he said, *"Everyting crisp. Pussy ole try an avenge him family."*

Dismissing his security, he reclined in his chair, asking himself what else could go wrong, and at that moment, Cashmere came in saying, "I have bad news."

*"Wah yuh have?"*

"Smitty's dead. He was found in his bed without a wound, but both his intestines were lying in his lap."

*"Wah typa fuckery dis?"*

"I don't understand, Ricky."

*"Don't worry yaself 'cause obiah kill him."*

# Chapter 7

# Six Months Later

"Good morning, handsome," said Tessa, waking up Divine with a kiss because she felt great since he'd unclogged her drain with his plunger last night.

"Damn, girl! Can I get some sleep?" he said, hiding his head underneath a pillow due to the bright light coming through their bedroom windows.

"I know you're tired. You need to rejuvenate, so eat this akee and salt fish, drink your carrot juice, then go back to sleep."

Coming up from underneath the pillow, he said, "That's what I'm talkin' 'bout," as he grabbed the tray of food.

"Oooh, boy, don't talk, just eat because I think I saw a fly come out of your stankin' ass mouth," she said, jokingly.

Not the one to be without a sense of humor, he closed his eyes, puckered his lips, and said, "Come and give me a kiss," in between bites of his food.

"When you brush," she said, as she sashayed out of their master bedroom, knowing his eyes were locked on her big bubble butt.

Enjoying his meal, he smiled because breakfast cooked after a night of freaking off was always an indicator that a man had pleased his woman. Lying in bed, he contemplated the last few steps to his plan over and over, making sure he had all angles covered. There was no room for error, so he pictured everything in his mind's eye, as if he was watching a movie. His thought remained on replay until she came back into the room saying, "Hey, handsome! It's time for you to get dressed because you have a business meeting."

"I quit!" he shouted, while groggily heading to the bathroom to wash up.

Getting dressed after a long shower, he figured out how he would get the ball to his plan rolling, so he said, "Bae, my luncheon will be over by 12:30 pm, so stop by, so we can have a bite together."

"What's the special occasion?"

"Love."

Blushing with butterflies fluttering in her stomach, she watched her man head for the door with the thoughts of being the luckiest woman on earth.

As she cleanied up their massive house, she smiled because she knew she had a good man who loved her and their kids, a man who would walk to the ends of the earth to provide for his family, a man who would make certain sacrifices in order to keep the household together, a man who made sure his woman was satisfied in every aspect that needed to be satisfied.

After her long day of cleaning, she soaked in their Jacuzzi to soothe her aching joints. The jets massaged her from head to toe as she scrubbed herself with a loofah. Gently caressing her soapy breasts, she felt the urge to let her hands wander, but she quickly decided against it, because she could have her baby scratch her itch after their lunch date, if need be.

After dressing in a two-piece pants suit by Donna Karan that accented her curves and putting on shoes by BCBG, she headed for the door to meet her baby, only stopping to put on her favorite perfume, White Diamonds.

***

While driving to his meeting, Divine knew what he was about to do was wrong, but his plan had to be executed one way or another. His meeting was with a girl his partner Mizzle said had aspirations of becoming a model. She was a pretty half-black, half-German army brat that was destined for the big screen, so he decided he was going to get her career started by placing her in some of their artists' videos, but only if she agreed to help him with his plan.

Meeting at Buffalo Wild Wings in Port Chester, New York, he waited for his future model. She came into the establishment strutting her stuff, making every woman in the sports bar cut their eyes with envy. Always the gentleman, he stood to greet her with an extended hand, saying, "Hi! How are you? I'm Divine, and you must be ..."

Cutting him off mid-sentence, she said, "Oh, my God! It's really you. I'm never washing my hand again!"

Smiling was the only way to ease her nerves, so he said, "It's cool. I'm only human."

"You're one of the men responsible for some of my favorite artists, so be patient with me."

"If you calm down and get down to business, you'll meet ya favorite artists soon. Now, let's try this again. I'm Divine, and you are?"

"Oh, I'm sorry. My name is Natasha."

"Okay, Natasha, listen carefully because I'll make you an official part of the Hot Wax family but only if you do me a small favor first."

Pausing before she spoke, she said, "I'll fuck you until you beg for mercy," with a seductive look in her eye.

"That's good to know, so I'll keep you in mind if I ever get divorced, but that's not what I need from you."

"Oh, I'm sorry," she said, embarrassed that she'd exposed her hand.

"Ya good so don't worry about that. All I need you to do is make my wife jealous. Can you do that?"

"Can I? Do pigs play in mud? I could do that with my eyes closed."

"Cool. When she comes, she'll more than likely park by my car, so I'll spot her. When I do, I'll need you to sit on my lap and caress my cheek."

"When are you expecting her?"

"She'll be here any minute," he said, and like clockwork, she pulled in beside his BMW M6.

Happy to see her baby, she waved, but it appeared he didn't see her, so she grabbed her Gucci bag and walked toward the table where he was seated. She was only a few feet away, so he pretended to be lost in conversation when he said, "Do ya thing, Tasha."

On cue, as if she were a seasoned actress, she got up and straddled him. This sultry movement hiked up her mini skirt, revealing a pink thong while she caressed his face and kissed his bald head.

Appalled by what was taking place in front of her, Tessa rushed to the table, pulling Natasha off her soon-to-be ex-husband, so she could confront who she thought was a cheater.

Spewing profanity, she said, "How could you do this to us, Divine? You dirty dick mothafucka, I'm going to kill your bank account!"

"Bae, let me explain because ya overreacting."

"Kiss my ass, Divine," she said, as she stormed off.

Grabbing his phone, he called Maniac Main and told him to put Natasha on the payroll and in Sincere's next video. Ecstatic from what she was hearing, Natasha jumped up and down, which gave him a nice view of her C-cups.

"Thank you for doin' a good job, and for that reason, we're gonna make a lot of money together. Now go on 'bout ya business."

"Thank you so much! And don't forget to call me when you get divorced," she said, winking at him.

Laughing at her remark, he headed toward his car, proud that things were working out as planned.

\*\*\*

Packing her belongings and those of the girls, Tessa was heartbroken, unaware of what to think because she never expected that such a thing would ever happen to her during this lifetime. The pain was unbearable, so with tears in her eyes, she stopped packing and sunk to the floor, dizzy from the effects of love.

Arriving at the house, Divine rushed to their master bedroom, but he didn't find her there. He, then, rushed off to each of the girls' bedrooms until he finally found her in B-G's room balled up on the floor, crying. His attempt to stoop over in order to hold her in his arms as an effort to console her was ended abruptly because he was met with a slap to the face that sent saliva flying across the room.

"How could you ruin our family, Divine?"

"I didn't. She's a new model for our videos. I was showin' her the role she was gonna be playing in Sincere's new video. I told you to meet me there, so do you honestly think, if I was havin' an affair, I would have her with me when I was expectin' you? Do I look or act stupid?"

"I hate you, Divine!"

"I love you, too, and that's why we need to make this work."

"It can't work."

"Why not?"

"Because I can't trust you, that's why."

"Yes, you can 'cause I wasn't cheatin'."

"It sure looked like cheating to me, and for that matter, I can't trust you. If I can't trust you, we can't be together."

"Tessa, don't act like that."

"Divine, we need some space for a little while, so I can figure out what it is I'm going to do."

"Space for what, so you could go and fuck that nigga?"

"What nigga are you talking about?"

"You know what nigga I'm talkin' 'bout. The nigga that whispered in your ear every time he saw you is who I'm talkin' 'bout. That's the nigga you didn't give any rhythm since there wasn't any turbulence in the relationship. But now that we're goin' through it ya gonna break out his number that you had stored under Pizza Hut for this rainy day. I ain't stupid!"

"Divine, you're losing your mind …The kids will be at your mother's house, and I'll be at my godsister's."

"That's the proof in the puddin'! Ya godsister is a jump off, so she's gonna have you jumpin' off to get me off ya mind."

"Grow up, Divine," she said, as she exited their mansion.

He knew he was wrong for putting her through the heartache, but he had to do what was necessary.

***

Unable to eat or sleep, Tessa bawled like a baby on her godsister's couch for a week straight. On this day, her godsister tried consoling her by telling her that things would be okay with time and that she should try to work things out or move forward, closing this chapter of her life.

She only knew Tessa's side of the story, so she wasn't quick to judge or go against Divine. Her second reason for not siding with Tessa was because she felt Divine was a good man who had possibly let the glitz and glamour of the entertainment world blind him. If this were true, she felt he was worth a second chance.

Voicing her opinion, she said, "I think you should give it another try because you love one another."

Hearing this only made Tessa cry harder, causing her to have drool hang from her lips as she said, "I love him with all my soul and being."

"I know, girl," said her godsister, as she put Tessa's head in her lap.

"I miss him," she said, as she dried her eyes, heading to the kitchen in search of something to eat. As she arrived in the kitchen, the door bell rang. Ding dong.

"Are you expecting anybody?" she asked from the kitchen.

"No."

Leaving the fridge door open, she headed to the front door, peeked through the peep hole, then asked, "Who is it?"

"Sergio's Pizza!" replied the delivery man. "I have a grilled chicken and cheese salad with garlic bread for a

Tessa, and an extra large, hot and spicy shrimp pasta with Alfredo sauce for the both of you, free of charge from a Divine."

"Look, girl! That man loves your funky ass. He's making sure you eat all the while y'all beefin'."

"I know, and he got my favorite."

"Un-huh, honey, that's our favorite."

"Since when did you like Alfredo sauce that didn't come out of a man's penis?" asked Tessa, jokingly.

"Watch your mouth, ho. It's been my favorite since I'm not the one paying for it."

Sharing a laugh lightened the mood, so her godsister opened the door to accept the food. From the looks on the delivery man's face, Tessa knew that she was looking a hot mess, so she ran into the kitchen, embarrassed, while her godsister grabbed the food, said "Thanks," then slammed the door in his face.

"What about my tip?" he shouted from the other side of the door.

"I know Divine very well, so I know he gave you a fifty," shouted Tessa from inside the apartment.

Knowing that she was telling the truth, he shrugged his shoulders and went about his business while they devoured the food.

\*\*\*

Two weeks without Divine was utter hell, and Tessa couldn't take it any more, so she decided to call him. Keeping her sanity was a difficult task, but the daily talks with the girls kept her sane since their bubbly voices and laughter kept a smile on her face. The love of the children and the fact that she loved their father was the reason she decided to call and give their marriage a second chance.

Calling him later that day, she asked, "How are you?" with nervousness apparent in her voice.

"I'm a'ight knowin' that you a'ight. I miss you, Tessa."

She missed him more than she could stand but refused to reveal her true feelings; therefore, she countered his statement, saying, "We need to talk. Do you think you'll be available, or will you be getting your bald head licked by your little hoochie?"

"Bae, stop it. You know I'll drop everythin' to be there with you, just name the place and time."

"Don't *bae* me! We're not friends, Divine. Meet me at Pat's Hubba Hubba at nine tonight."

"I'll be there."

"You better be on time because, if I'm there before you, that will tell me you don't value an attempt at salvaging your marriage."

"When have you known me to be late?"

"Bye, Divine," she said, knowing he had a spell on her that had her so blinded by love she'd take him back no matter what he did.

"Tessa?"

"What?"

"I love you."

"Bye, Divine."

***

"What's good, homie?" asked Divine, as he spoke to his mystery friend.

"I'm good, B. I'm gettin' my dick sucked by ya old infamous head bop lady. She the truth!" said the mystery man.

"I need you, son."

"I got you. Just say the word."

"Nine o'clock at Pat's Hubba Hubba."

"Say no more."

"Make it authentic as possible, so I'll be expecting a call by nine forty-five."

"No doubt … you ain't got to school me 'cause I been doin' this since before Jesus turned water to wine."

Laughing at the mystery man's humor, he said, "Be easy."

"No doubt," said the mystery man, as the phone slipped from his fingers due to the marvelous job the head bop lady was doing.

***

Getting dressed in a pair of Nike Air Max sneakers, Baby Phat jeans, and a sweater, she opted to walk to Hubba Hubba's to enjoy the night's breeze and to possibly get over the butterflies in her stomach.

Talking aloud to herself, she said, "Woman up, girl! You're acting as if you just met this nigga, walking around feeling like a school girl. You've been in the bathroom while he was shittin' and kissed him before he brushed his teeth, so there's no reason to be nervous."

Lost in the conversation with herself, she didn't see the man in all black attire come out from behind an elm tree with a silenced semi-automatic handgun. Slipping behind her, the masked man placed the nozzle of the silencer in between two of her ribs, saying, "If you breathe too loud ya dead, so be a good girl, keep quiet, and head toward that black SUV."

Frozen with fear, she wished Divine was running late to save her, but she knew that was a wasted wish, because he was never late, never on time, but always early to a rendezvous. Following instructions, she opened the back door and sat on the passenger side. Laying her down, the masked man gagged her mouth, blindfolded her, and hog-tied her, then strapped her in with a safety belt.

Hopping onto I-95 south, heading to I-287, he drove in silence until he reached the backwoods of Armonk, New York. He cruised the backroads, coming to a complete stop at stop signs, and obeyed every other motor vehicle law as if he was a law-abiding, working-class citizen.

Finally reaching a lake front cabin, he carried her into a living room where he taped her to a chair. Then he dialed Divine's number from a throw away phone.

\*\*\*

"Ring, ring, ring, ring" sounded off on Divine's phone, as he looked at the caller ID which displayed a blocked number. Letting the call go through to voicemail, he took shots of Remy Martin XO, followed by swigs of Guinness as a chaser. When he replayed the message on the speaker phone, he heard, "Congratulations, Mr. Big Wig Record

Executive! You've been lucky enough to win my raffle. What did you win, you ask? You've won the opportunity to prove your love by paying me ten million cash to get your lovely wife back. Ain't that right, Tessa?" asked the kidnapper, as he ungagged her mouth, so she could speak.

Given the opportunity to speak, she said, "Baby, help me! I don't want to die! Help me, Divine!"

"Now you know this ain't a game. Have my money if you want your pretty piece of pussy back. One more thing, Divine. No police! If I think you're thinking about contacting the police, I'll cut her head off and go bowling with it, then leave it on YouTube for the world to see," he said. Then, he hung up the phone.

Ending the voicemail, he felt a knot form in his stomach, so he threw back the rest of the Remy to drink away the pain.

***

Humming the melody to his favorite tune, the kidnapper placed the gag back on Tessa's mouth because he didn't want to hear her cry. Removing his mask, he popped a bottle of Patrón to congratulate himself with a shot, then put the mask back on, and said, "I'm going to remove your blindfold, so you're not in the dark, but if you piss me off, I'll be more than glad to kill your pretty ass … do you understand me?"

Wanting to say yes, she said, "Hmm," through her gag.

"I don't speak gag, so nod your head up and down for yes and and shake it left to right for no."

Catching his drift, she nodded her head up and down to indicate she understood what was just said, even though she was scared shitless. Removing the blindfold let in rays of bright light that made her squint, making it hard to adjust her vision. Once her eyes adjusted, she looked around for something familiar, but at that moment, the kidnapper spoke, saying, "Baby girl, I've been abducting people for a long time, so I'm not new to this. If you don't understand what I mean by that, it means you could look around for signs to try and figure out where you are, but you won't find any."

Walking back over to where he placed the bottle of Patrón, he poured two shots. One for himself, and one for her as he said, "Take a shot of this. It will calm your nerves."

Placing the shot in front of her, he said, "I'm going to remove your gag, so you can have your drink and only your drink. If you scream, I will knock out three of your front teeth with no fear of getting caught because nobody can hear you out here. I will not knock your teeth out in fear of being apprehended but for the mere reason of you pushing my button. I'm not here to hurt you, and I won't as long as you follow my orders. Do you understand?"

Nodding her head up and down with lightning speed, she dared not aggravate this man, because she didn't think he was bluffing. Removing the gag, he placed the shot glass to her mouth because he wasn't going to untie her hands. He then placed a finger under her chin, gently tilting her head backward, so he could pour the tequila down her throat. She took it back straight, with no chaser, grimaced from the burn, then asked, "May I have another?"

Pouring another shot, he said, "As long as you behave, I'll treat you like my guest of honor who'll be going back to their lovely family shortly."

Swallowing the second shot gave her the strength to ask, "Why are you doing this?"

"I do what I'm paid to do … I don't ask why," he said, as he gagged her mouth again.

Picking up the chair along with her, he carried her to the kitchen until they reached the kitchen's island. Unaware of what was going on, she closed her eyes, petrified, in fear of being executed. Having had been gently placed down, she opened her eyes to find him going into the refrigerator. He turned around, pulling out green bell peppers, scallions, jalapeño peppers for heat, and salmon steaks. He then reached into a cupboard and pulled out basmati rice, salt, black pepper, Maggi boullion cubes, garlic cloves, vegetable oil, and a can of tomato paste. Slicing the green peppers and scallions as the vegetable oil heated in a skillet, he asked, "Are you hungry?"

Although she was as hungry as a slave, she was reluctant to say "yes" because she feared being poisoned.

Sensing her fear, he said, "If I wanted to kill you, I wouldn't waste poison on you, so just enjoy the meal because I'm an excellent chef."

Watching him closely, she noticed that he took care to wash his hands whenever he handled different foods in an attempt to prevent cross contamination. The smell of green peppers, garlic, scallions, and Maggi filled the room as they sautéed in the skillet. He threw in touches of salt and pepper, along with tomato paste, to make a sauce, and the savory aromas made her mouth water. Seeing that he took pride in his cooking, she thought to herself, If tonight is my night to die, I'll, at least, have a last supper. Forty-five minutes later, food was served to her on the counter of the kitchen's island.

Untying her right hand, so she could eat, he placed a plastic fork in front of her, then stepped off to the side to see if she liked it. Watching his movement, she tried to look deep into his eyes because she felt deep inside that this was a compassionate man who wouldn't harm her, unless he was forced to. His gaze never met hers, so she gave up, then diverted her attention to the meal in front of her. Fear gave her the appetite of an entire football team, so she went to work, cleaning her plate. Seeing this, he felt good inside because he took pride in his cooking. He also hoped that whatever it was Divine was doing was worth the trauma that kidnap victims endured for years down the line.

*\*\*\**

Playing the voice mail over and over, Divine's heart hurt because he loved Tessa deeply. Although he hurt, he put his feelings aside to prevent allowing love to cloud his judgment because keeping his focus was imperative in these final stages of his plan. Lost in thought, he let the voice mail play for two hours while sitting in the dark behind the console in his nightmare studios. Snapping out of his daze, he finally turned off the recording, then dialed a number to the West Indies, so he could reach Tessa's only other emergency contact.

Picking up the phone on the third ring, Ricky asked, *"Who a call from foreign?"*

"It's me. Divine."

"*Mi neva know him,*" he said, as he prepared to hang up.

Frustrated because the bastard hadn't made an attempt to remember his name, Divine spoke through clenched teeth, saying, "*Di DJ, my yout.*"

"*Wha gwon, DJ?*"

"Ricky, we need to talk."

"*We nah affi chat 'bout nothin'! Mi hear yu still vexed from when yu com a yard.*"

"That's old news, Ricky. I didn't want to call you, so don't try to grand stand. The only reason I'd possibly call you is for help."

"*My help ... hmmm. It a cost a whole heap a money 'cause bad mon nah par wit' pussy ole,*" he said, with scorn because he never felt Divine was good enough for his princess Tessa.

"Mothafuck you, you bitch-ass nigga!" he shouted, while pacing around his studio.

*"Bwoy, yu know who yu a romp wit'?"*

"Shut the fuck up, Ricky! I let them things fly for real, but I'm not 'bout to bicker with you 'bout who's the bigger gangsta. I called you to tell you that Tessa, ya daughter, been kidnapped. My people ain't come up with the source of the kidnapper's location, so do you want to go back and forth 'bout whose dick bigger, or do you want to help me find my wife?"

Staring at the phone in disbelief that Divine would speak to him in such a way, and for the fact that he heard something that sounded like his baby girl had been abducted, he gripped the handle of his old school Colt .45 caliber hand cannon, then asked, *"DJ, yu sey wha!?"*

"Yes, Ricky, you heard right. Tessa's been kidnapped, but I don't know by who. All I know is that we were supposed to meet for a dinner, but she never showed up. I waited for half an hour, but she never came, so I left for home, half-expectin' to see her there, but she wasn't there either. We were working out a few problems, so I didn't think nothin' of it; therefore, I started workin' on a few tracks in my studio, causing me not to hear when my phone rang with the kidnapper's call. When I wrapped up my session, I noticed I had voice mails, so I checked my messages, expectin' to hear her apologizing for standing me up, but I heard what I thought was a joke of a ransom call until I heard her voice begging for me to come to her rescue."

*"DJ, mi nah g' play dem typa game, so tell mi whey mi pitny."*

"What didn't you understand about what I just said? My wife's somewhere scared to death, yet, you think I want to play *Tom and Jerry* cat and mouse games with you!" he shouted, trying to get his point across.

*"Really an' truly, DJ?"*

"Shut up and listen," he said, as he put his cell phone on speaker to play the ransom call aloud for Ricky to hear.

None of the message meant anything to him until he heard the pleas of his only daughter. Anger wasn't the word for what he felt at that moment. He was irate, causing the blood in his veins to boil like mercury above a flame in a thermometer. He knocked over lamps, his computer and a ten-thousand-dollar portrait of Bob Marley, then stormed around his office, in an attempt to vent. He followed this tirade with several shots of Wray and Nephew white rum. But it was a wasted attempt at calming his nerves, so he shouted, "*Mi a kill a baga mon a foreign fi every blood clot minute mi princess gone!*"

"We gonna have to put the bullshit to the side and work together day and night until we find her."

"*Yu nah affi worry yaself, DJ. Everyting crisp,*" he said, as he hung up the phone.

Sitting behind his console, he was shocked to be listening to a dial tone because Ricky didn't say whether they were going to work together, let alone if he was coming at all.

***

*"Call Sleepy an di massive an tell dem tek all di machine dem cuz we a go foreign an mash up di blood clot. No question asked, yu hear me?"* said Ricky, shouting orders to Cashmere.

"Am I taking this trip, too?" she asked.

*"Cum no, gyal,"* he said, as he rushed out of his office, heading to his private G5 jet.

Once the whole crew arrived at the hangar, he told them that this was a risky situation because his daughter was in danger, and that the dilemma they faced was in the States, where he didn't have political ties to keep him safe from the long arm of the law, whose grip he'd managed to evade for the last thirty years.

Hearing this, both Sleepy and Cashmere volunteered to go in his absence, but he wanted to hear nothing of it since it was personal. After turning down their offer, he said, *"We a g' foreign an we nah g' play no games! Gunshot pon dem! Mi pitny dis so mi cyant sit back an' watch ... see mi?"*

Everyone agreed in silence, then bowed their heads while he said a prayer for which would be the first time some of them stepped off the island and for forgiveness for the sins they were about to commit. Acting as if she was praying, Cashmere promised to find a spare minute to stop by her one and only true love K-Blizz's grave site while she was in the States to ask for his forgiveness and to apologize because she felt incomplete without love, even though she had a world of money.

\*\*\*

"Where's my money, Mr. Record Executive? Do you really love your wife? If so, act like it by delivering by money to Vidal Court Houses. You have seventy-two hours to have my money in non-sequential bills delivered to my partner in the inside stair case on the fifth floor of Building 52," said the kidnapper.

"You better not hurt her, you bastard!" yelled Divine into the phone's receiver.

"Calm down now. I don't want you to have a heart attack before you pay up, so settle your nerves and remember that her life's in your hands, not mine ... cheerio!"

Hitting the stop button on his recorder, Divine headed to his mother's house to see his little girls, but he was stopped short in mid-stride when he saw a West Indies number on the display screen of his phone.

Quickly answering, he heard someone with a thick Jamaican accent say, "*Dis di DJ?*"

"Yes, who this?"

"*Nuff a di small chat. Yu hav any information fi Ricky?*"

"I just got off the phone with the kidnapper, and I recorded everything that was said, so if he wants to help me get my wife back, I'll keep him in the loop by sharin' my newly found information," he said, baiting whoever he was on the phone with.

"*Cool it, DJ. No one wan' Tessa back more dan Ricky, so sen mi di record.*"

"Hang up but don't answer when I call back, so I can leave it on your voice mail."

"Cool," said the man on the other end of the phone before hanging up.

Being true to his word, he called right back and left the recording on the voice mail in hopes of it reaching

Ricky in order to provoke him away from his comfort zone on the tropical island of Jamaica to the United States where he would be vulnerable enough to be caught slipping. Hanging up the phone, he headed to his mother's house unaware that Ricky was already in flight and only had an hour and a half left before he stepped foot in the States.

***

After a long flight, they landed at a friend's privately-owned air strip that could accommodate Cessnas but nothing bigger than Ricky's G5. When he stepped onto the tarmac, he barked orders to his team of fifteen cold-blooded murderers. His team of henchmen stood strong individually, so he had faith in them. Therefore, he broke them into three teams of five. Loading their weapons, the men joked about how big of a bonus their individual team would get if they were the ones to find the kidnapper.

Putting one in the air to calm his nerves, Ricky paced back and forth, awaiting a fleet of armored Cadillac Escalades to keep him and the team out of harm's way. Burning his big head spliff, he felt good, knowing he had a loyal team that was willing to go to war with the American military, if he gave the order to do so. Interrupting his thoughts was the fleet of four heavily armored Escalades, which every team of five hopped into, leaving one for him and Cashmere.

Sleepy's team was the first off on the mission to blow up Vidal Court Houses in search of Tessa's kidnappers, while the other two teams followed the boss to some of his old stomping grounds. Feeling a vibe that something wasn't right, Ricky looked over at Cashmere, who was staring out of the window, oblivious to his gaze, to tell her that something didn't feel right, but her stunning beauty made the feeling disappear. Admiring her smooth skin, full lips, and voluptuous breasts, he sang a new tune, disregarding his gut instinct, *"Long time mi nah foreign."*

\*\*\*

"Daddy!" shouted Trinity and Divinity, as they ran toward him to give a bear hug.

Falling to the ground, giving the impression they knocked him down, he said, "You girls are getting bigger and stronger every day. You knocked me down with ease."

"Look, Daddy, I have mus-cles," said Divinity, as she made her best attempt at flexing her muscle.

"What's good with you, Dad?" asked B-G, as she sized him up, as if she wanted to throw hands.

"B-G is only your nickname. Ya not really a gangsta, so stop tryin' to play me like a chump, Serenity," he said, pushing her buttons.

Gasping for air in shock, she asked, "What you wanna do?" as she threw her hands up.

Finding this little spectacle amusing, he smiled because her little fists were cute and because this was their unique way of bonding. A little boxing between them would lead to him tickling her until she squealed like a little pig. Knowing what was in store, he sucker-punched her lightly as he said, "Nana wants you."

Catching her completely off guard, she was dazed, so he put her in a headlock, then laid on the floor. Today wasn't going to be all in his favor because she had back up when both Trinity and Divinity jumped in to rescue their little sister. What told him that he couldn't win was his mother jumping in, saying, "Get off my, grandbaby."

While rolling around on the floor with four of his five ladies, he savored the moment, and they played for the next four hours.

*** 

Entering Vidal Court Houses, slowly going over speed bumps, Sleepy looked for building numbers from behind tinted windows as chicks, hustlers, and gangstas looked with curiosity at the unfamiliar SUV.

Finding Building 52, he double-parked and left the motor running as his team jumped out one by one, equipped with Kel-Tec assault rifles. New to the United States but never new to the hood, Sleepy knew a few a young boys were scheming on taking a joyride, so he hit the automatic lock on the key chain to lock the doors, although the truck was still running. As they headed for the elevator, they stepped over Dutchie guts, empty bottles of Hennessy, and puddles of piss, so Sleepy said, "*Dis a di foreign ghetto!*"

Pushing up on the elevator's control panel, Sleepy told two members of his team to take the stairs. One member was to stay on the bottom floor, so there was somebody holding down the ground floor. Then the last member of his team took the elevator. It was this team member's job to hold the elevator, so they'd have a quick way down.

Seeing how slow and raggedy the elevator was on the ride up, Sleepy made a mental note not to use it if a hasty retreat was needed. Stepping off the elevator and to his right, he spotted a guy who went by the name of Ray-Ro getting head from a young girl at the top of the staircase. Realizing he had the drop, he slowly moved on his unsuspecting victim who was on cloud nine because the young girl was already a professional at sucking some cock at the tender age of sixteen. She was a beast because he wouldn't penetrate her young ass, but to please her, he would suck every ounce of fluid out of her tender and tight pussy.

Placing the nozzle of his fully automatic assault rifle at the nape of Ray's neck, Sleepy said, *"Whey di gyaal dey?"*

Known to joke a lot, Ray thought it was his right-hand man Shit-Shit, so he said, "Get the fuck out of here before I pull out and nut on ya leg."

*"Hey, pussy ole Yankee bwoy, bad mon yu par wit so cool yaself,"* said Sleepy, as he went across Ray's head and opened up a two-inch gash from the pistol whipping.

Completely unaware of what was going on due to being in her zone, the young girl sucked and swallowed his shaft with her eyes closed, imagining his cock was nutty coconut ice cream from Baskin Robbins.

Seeing that shit was getting thick, Ray tried to reach for his chrome P90 Ruger, but one of Sleepy's men let a shot ring out, hitting him right in the hand because he had bad intentions. Hearing the shot and Ray yell out in pain, the young girl slowly opened her eyes, just to be scared shitless by the sight of his hand and the looks of sheer terror in the eyes of these heavily armed strangers. Never afraid of speaking her mind when she had an issue, the girl sang "help" in such a high octave that dogs in surrounding neighborhoods jumped up at attention. Knowing the gunshot and her cry for help would alarm the projects that some bullshit had done popped off, Sleepy sprayed two shots into her mouth, blowing her head clean off right before asking Ray for Tessa's whereabouts one more time. Scared and confused, he responded by saying, "I don't know Tessa."

"*Lie yu tell.*"

"I'm serious! This is where I hustle, and I'm here every day, but I don't know no Tessa."

"*All right. Mi sorry mi bodda yu,*" he said, as he looked around at the members of his team, indicating it was time to off him and make their retreat. As if on cue, they riddled his body with forty bullets. Ten from each of their weapons, making his body dance its last ever Harlem Shake.

Hearing the shots, the niggas out on the strip grabbed their ratchets and headed toward Building 52, only to be met by a barrage of bullets by the team member that had remained on the ground floor.

Ducking behind parked cars in the housing complex's open-air garage, they exchanged fire with the intruder to their hood. Slugs whizzed by heads and shattered windshields to parked vehicles. Adrenaline coursed through veins as residents rushed to slam doors shut against the projectiles.

Sticking his head over the railing, Sleepy spotted the groups of his attackers, so he fired a succession of shots from his vantage point five stories above. Granting his team coverage, they took off down the stairs, heading for the SUV. Ducking extra low behind the vehicles in fear of losing their heads, they reached over the hoods and roofs of cars firing blindly in what they thought was Sleepy's direction. What saved them from Sleepy's bird's-eye view was the fact that somebody was always in the staircases in all of the buildings at all times. Coming out of an elevator in fifty-two was the hood reinforcements, who spotted Sleepy, then commenced to bang on him.

Across from the madness taking place in Building 52, a few young boys on the sixth floor of Building 74's outside staircase were smoking dust juice dipped cigarettes, so they started firing shots in Sleepy's direction, also, making him run for cover. Shots whizzed by his head, breaking windows and chipping off pieces of red brick.

*"Jesus Christ! Dem bwoy a foreign gangsta!"* he said, with a smile on his face as he took the stairs down by fours. Hitting the ground floor, he spotted two of his team members reloading while the others sent shots through the air to keep their attackers at bay.

Unaware of the basement and what took place down there, Sleepy and his men didn't notice the stairs that led to it, and that would prove to be fatal. The two members of Sleepy's team that had reloaded their weapons took the front line with him closely on their heels as the other two played the rear. Firing shots at anything moving, Sleepy was protected by his entourage's defense, so he hit the automatic unlock on the remote to open the doors of the SUV because that was considered to be their home base where nothing could harm them.

They rushed off to the truck, but one of the first two members got legged in the process yet still managed to climb in, put it in gear, and drive onto the sidewalk up to the hallway opening where the elevator was located, blocking the line of fire of their attackers. Bullets pinged off the SUV as all but one man dove through the truck's open doors.

"*Cum no, mon!*" yelled the driver, but his words fell on deaf ears because his comrade's chest opened up with a hole the size of a mango as a shotgun blast from behind took his life.

Falling to his knees in shock, he put his fingers into the hole in his chest before he fell forward, revealing a masked man who had crept up from behind by way of the basement. Brandishing a Mossberg shotgun and a hunger for more victims, the masked man quickly fired two more shots in the direction of the open doors, but they were quickly pulled shut as someone in the truck said, "*Tek off no, mon!*"

Skidding off the curb, slugs hit the truck like raindrops in a torrential downpour as niggas from the hood squeezed the triggers on AKs, ARs, Macs and anything else they had within hand's reach.

Rushing over speed bumps, they shot out of the complex like bats out of hell and headed back to Ricky's friend's air hangar to inform him of what had taken place. Riding off as quiet as an empty church, they said a prayer for their fallen comrade.

***

"All right. Now keep it down because we've had enough play time, so go wash up and get ready for supper," said Chantal to Divine and her three granddaughters.

Obeying the orders given, everyone washed up then seated themselves back at the table where the food was being served. Taking their seats, they watched the evening news, surprised to see a breaking news bulletin with the reporter saying, "This just in ... there's been a gun battle in the Vidal Court Houses, leaving three dead. One adult black male riddled with thirty or more bullets, an underage black female who suffered two gunshots to the head, and another black male who was shot from behind, through the sternum. All the bodies were found in the building behind

332

me known as 'Fifty-Two' to the residents of the complex. There's a substantial amount of property damage, ranging in the hundreds of thousands, so the community is outraged. This is all the information we have for now, but we will keep you informed as soon as we know more. This is Bob Ellsworth reporting live from the Vidal Court Houses on Channel Eleven News, back to you, Theresa."

"Got damn gang bangers make me sick," said Chantal, disgusted with the news she just saw.

In shock, Divine didn't hear his phone ring, so the caller left a message. He was lost in thought, trying to figure out the next step in his plan because he knew that what happened tonight was Ricky's work. Excusing himself from the dining room table, he went to the bathroom to check his voice mail, which contained a message saying, "You think that was cute, huh? Well, I'm gonna show you cute when I send you ya wife's finger gift wrapped in a beautiful package. Ya tryin' my patience, and that's not wise, so I suggest you don't do that again, unless you want me to chop her up until there's nothing left but her pussy. You'd like that, right? Deliver my money to the beach at Southfield Park at one o'clock am."

After hanging up, Divine called the West Indies number that was in his phone log and relayed the message. But only after he voiced he was upset that Ricky had not contacted him to let him know his whereabouts.

\*\*\*

*"Ricky, whey yu dey?"* asked Sleepy through the phone's receiver.

*"Mi see pon di news yu mash up di place. Wha yu hav fi mi?"* said Ricky.

*"Ricky, we nah hav nothin. Di Yankee bwoy swear pon him madda him neva know Tessa. Furthermore, we lost Scooby."*

*"Cool yaself 'cause we hav' tonight. We a send Green Eye an dem,"* said Ricky, as he hung up the phone.

Sitting down at a table with Cashmere at the Caribbean Bakery located at what the locals call the Purple Bridge, they ate stew chicken and drank cola champagne while he brought her up to speed on the current events. After she was caught up, she told him she was going to need some time to go to the cemetery before they returned to Jamaica, and he, being a man of compassion, told her to go tomorrow after they got the night over with. Thanking him, even though she was going with or without his consent, she gave him a hug, then whispered in his ear, "I know I just ate, but I'm not full, so can you fill my belly with that long, thick cock of yours."

Feeling the warm breath on his ear while her words registered, he began to get a hard-on, making him quickly pay the bill, grab her by the waist, jump in the truck, and head downtown to the Marriot Courtyard.

***

Later that night, Green Eyes and three of his team sat in a dinghy, floating in the pitch-black waters of the Long Island Sound because it washed up on the shores of Southfield Park's beach. Awaiting their mark, they all looked at their watches to find that it was only 10:30 pm. The cash drop was supposed to be made at one in the morning, so they had ample time for surveillance.

Equipped with night vision binoculars, silenced assault rifles, and oxygen tanks, Green Eyes and his clique floated in the water as they kept a vigilant watch on everything moving while the fifth member of his team was designated to be the drop man. He wasn't there yet, but he was very close to the drop sight.

At 12:30 am on the dot, a rust-colored Range Rover Sport pulled into the parking lot and what looked like a young hustler jumped out, carrying two Louis Vuitton suitcases. One, filled with cocaine, and the other with silencers. He was unaware of the goon squad floating in the sound behind him.

Waiting approximately forty minutes after the young hustler's arrival, Green Eyes's fifth team member pulled into the parking lot, parking a few spaces away, allowing himself room, just in case a gun battle erupted. Stepping out of the armored Cadillac Escalade, carrying two duffel bags of what was supposed to be money, he walked toward the young hustler, who pulled out his P89 Ruger as he asked, "Who that? What you doing over here? You know the park closed at sunset, right?"

"I'm here to see you for DJ," said the fifth member, in his best English. He was the perfect man for the job of avoiding suspicion because he spoke great English. He had lived in the States for twelve years before getting deported.

The young hustler knew something was wrong because he wasn't there to meet anybody by the name of

337

DJ. His contact's name was Steezo, so because he was a scary nigga, he automatically popped two shots into the man carrying the duffel bags.

Watching this whole ordeal unravel, Green Eyes cursed under his breath as his man hit the ground. Witnessing this, he and two others began to fire shots at the young hustler as the last remaining soldier dove into the black water in an attempt to come from the hustler's blind side.

Ducking as shots whizzed by his head, he knew shit wasn't a game because he didn't hear the loud sound of shots, but he sure did hear them zinging by as they hit parked cars and trees. Needing time to evaluate what was going on, he screwed on a silencer, then banged shots in the direction he thought the shots came from in hopes of hitting his target. Finding it to be senseless, firing shots at an invisible target, both the young hustler and Green Eyes's team stopped firing because they both were dealing with a silent enemy. The difference between these opposing forces was that Green Eyes had an advantage because he had night vision binoculars.

Making due with street sense, the young hustler fired two shots in hopes of spotting nozzle flashes, so he could have a general idea of where his attackers were. His plan panned out because he spotted their location but only after one of their hot ones plugged him in the shoulder. Because he was a person who ran from his problems, he knew it was time to go, so he hit automatic start on his Range, and the head lights came on, and they were so bright that they blinded Green Eyes and his entourage, giving him clean shots that he didn't hesitate to take. His shots hit the two soldiers on the dinghy, dead center, in their heads, sending them spilling over into the Sound. Ironically, his last two shots hit Green Eyes in the eyes, leaving him to float in the dinghy on Long Island Sound.

Assuming the coast was clear, he picked up his suitcases, then placed them in the Range. He then laid his head on the window to clear his mind and calm down, but his calm didn't last long because, out of nowhere, he felt a cold, wet barrel on his right temple.

"Take the coke and the silencers in the suitcases. Just don't hurt me. I don't have any beef with y'all."

"*Whey di gyal Tessa? Whey yu partner a keep her?*"

"I don't know what ya talkin' 'bout. I'm here to off three bricks and some silencers, and that's it."

"*Mi sorry to hear dat if yu a tell di trut,*" said the gunman right before he splattered the hustler's brain on the windshield with two shots to the temple from close range.

After grabbing the suitcases that the young hustler had brought to the scene first, he then searched his boy's pockets for the keys to the Escalade. After he found them, he took off into the night.

\*\*\*

"I heard you tell my husband to drop the money off, so why haven't I been set free?" asked Tessa.

"Your husband thinks he's Rambo, pretty lady. He's gotten it into his mind that he can get my partners at the drop sites to tell him your whereabouts. For that fact, you're going to call him to tell him that I will kill you if anything like what has happened at the other drop sites happens again. Do you understand?" said the kidnapper, as he dialed Divine's home number.

Recognizing that the only blocked number that called his home was the kidnapper, Divine quickly pressed record on his answering machine before he picked up the phone and said, "Hello."

"Mr. Record Executive, your disregard for your wife's life amazes me, so let me make sure you understand that this is not a fuckin' game!" shouted the kidnapper, as he fired a single shot into the air, causing Tessa to scream out of fear.

"I'll kill you, bastard," said Divine through clenched teeth.

"It's only a flesh wound to the leg, so she'll be all right as long as you deliver my money. I'm a good shot, and it looks like I hit the main artery, so you have a limited amount of time to bring my cash before she bleeds to death."

Feeling defeated, Divine said, "Okay. I'll have the money. Just don't hurt her."

"That's a good boy. The drop site is Carwin Park on Spruce Street at two in the morning."

"I'll be there with ya money. Just don't hurt her. Now let me speak to her," said Divine, but instead of hearing her sweet voice, he heard a dial tone.

\*\*\*

Lil Haiti

"*Hey, Ricky! Di bwoy kill off alla di massive but yu nah affi worry yaself cuz mi done him,*" said the fifth and only surviving soldier of Green Eyes's team.

"*Wha typa fuckery dis? Yu stay like yu a bad mon but yu let one pussy ole Yankee kill off a baga bad mon! G'way from here so!*" shouted Ricky.

Never the one to have much love for Ricky or the way he talked to people, he thought the three bricks and silencers were exactly what he needed to leave the organization, so that was exactly what he did.

***

"Playboy, what's good?" asked Divine, as they sat at a Haitian restaurant on Elm Street by the name of Lacaye.

"I'm good. What's good with you? I see a look in your eyes I ain't seen in years," said Playboy.

343

Bringing his boy up to speed about Tessa's kidnapping, Divine told him about the drop that was planned for later that night and that he had a plan that would enable him to slump all of Ricky's henchmen.

"Let's do it," said Playboy, who was always down for whatever.

"You'll take Colman Towers on the ninth floor and Swiss will take the third floor of the Martin Luther King building. There'll be a 30.06 assault rifle waiting for both of you in the apartments, giving you guys a bird's-eye view and coverage of both sides of the park. My signal to squeeze will be when I bend down to pick up the duffel bags."

"We got you!" said Playboy, as they ate and went over their plan.

\*\*\*

"This is almost over Tessa, so don't do anything to work the one nerve I have," said the kidnapper.

Looking at him, she knew he wouldn't hurt her because he had used a scare tactic on Divine to make him think she was suffering from a potentially deadly gunshot wound, rather than injuring her. She also knew that she was his leverage, so she remained calm, awaiting the day she'd be reunited with her kids and husband who she regretted walking out on. Missing Divine like crazy and appreciative of everything he was doing to get her back safely, she promised to make their bond stronger than ever once they were reunited. Unaware of where she mustered the words, she said, "Divine's going to kill you."

"Ha-ha," laughed the kidnapper, before saying, "I highly doubt that."

"You'll see," she said, with venom dripping from every word.

"You can't kill who you don't know," he said, as he gagged her mouth.

\*\*\*

Unable to contact Ricky, Divine left the recording he got from the kidnapper on the king of Jamaica's voicemail, then said, "What type of shit you on? Ya daughter's missin', all types of chaos is transpiring with no results, and you yet to come see me. Do you even care about her safety? I don't think so because ya goon squad is the reason my wife is bleedin' to death from a gunshot wound to the leg."

Satisfied with the recording he left, he hung up and headed to his studio to clear his mind. Taking a seat behind the mix board, he looked up at the flat screen mounted on the wall and noticed a female was entering the mausoleum where his father, Blizz, and Rob were buried.

Witnessing this, he smiled to himself. Then he said, "She finally came to pay her respects, huh?"

*⁎*

"*Sleepy, whey yu dey?*" asked Ricky, through the phone's receiver.

"*Mi neva too far fi yu, boss.*"

"*Good ... mi need fi yu tek di massive to a park dem call Carwin pon Spruce Street.*"

"*Wha time yu sey, boss?*"

"*Two in a thee mornin. Yu hav it?*"

"*Yeah, mon.*"

"All right," said Ricky, as he hung up the phone.

Sitting in the dark confines of his hotel room, he asked himself what was going on and where was Cashmere, so he picked up his phone to dial her number. There was no response, giving him no choice but to leave a message, saying, "*Miss Pretty-Pretty, whey yu dey? We affi chat.*"

\*\*\*

Stepping into the mausoleum, Cashmere's stomach was in knots because nervous was an understatement to what she was feeling. Just knowing that she was the cause of her true love's death would eventually drive her crazy, so she came to his grave site to ask for his forgiveness.

Running her fingers over his name, she cried from knowing that she'd never be able to hold him in the morning, feel his stroke, hear his laugh, or play with his chest hairs while he slept ever again, so speaking through tears and sobs, she said, "Blizz, I'm sorry. I don't know what got into me that night, and because of what I did, I've been on a one-way path to self-destruction."

Lil Haiti

Breaking down to her lowest, she bawled like a baby for a while without caring whether she lived or not. She was in emotional anguish, so she didn't notice the little black camera that watched her like a bird of prey. Her absentmindedness would prove to be a very unwise move, especially for someone like her who knew the rules to the game.

"Blizz, I miss you! I wish I could take that night back. I wish we could've settled down together to raise a family. I would've given you the two boys and two girls you wanted, and they would've been more than adorable. This has been so hard for me. I've been putting my life in danger for years in hopes that someone would me out of my misery, but I'm still here suffering. Pulling that trigger was the worst mistake of my life because I love you, I miss you, and I'm haunted by the look of shock in your eyes. I know you're in heaven looking down on me with disgust, but I need you to believe me when I say I'm sorry."

Rising to her feet, feeling a little better, she read the names of the other people laid to rest in the mausoleum, spotting Robbery Rob first, then Joseph Jean-Baptiste next. And that was when things began to make sense in her world but not with what was really going on in reality. Her mind was clouded by love, and she lacked the specifics of Ricky's past, so she missed the moment of clarity that could've benefited her in the long run.

Joseph's name made her think of Divine, so it clicked that he was the same Divine who Blizz considered to be a brother. For confirmation, she reached into her Louis bag in search of Sincere's album jacket, and she saw Divine Jean-Baptiste clear as day as the executive producer of the album. Recalling old conversations she'd shared with Blizz, she could hear him talking about a Divine that she never got to meet until recently. This, to her, was a sign of forgiveness because she felt the Lord put Divine into her life as a peace offering from Blizz. Divine and a few others were like brothers to him, so she believed that she now had a piece of her lost love.

She felt like a weight had melted from her heart and shoulders, so she said,

"Thank you for forgiving me, baby."

"Ya welcome," said Divine, as he stood, pointing a double-barrel shotgun in her direction.

Spinning around quick on the draw, the fragile woman that he had just witnessed crying and begging for forgiveness vanished and turned back into what she really was — a snake, so he let off a shot, which tore off the shin bone of her left leg. The blast rattled her world, and the gun flew out of her hand as she fell to the ground. She hit the ground in gut-wrenching pain, shouting obscenities.

Walking toward her, he stood over her, then said, "You killed two of my brothers, and ya boss killed my father, so you both gotta die."

"I loved Blizz, Divine!"

"Killin' the man you love is a weird way of showin' him."

"Fuck you! I don't have to explain shit to you!"

"I know. I didn't want to hear it, and you wouldn't have been alive long enough to complete the story anyway," he said, as he put the barrel to her head, then squeezed, blowing her melon clean off.

"Hey, Blizz ... I love you. Swiss loves you. T-Gunz loves you, and Playboy loves you so fuck that raggedy bitch! The same goes for you, Rob," he said, as he departed from the mausoleum.

***

Giving orders like a drill sergeant, Sleepy had the rest of his team's full attention and cooperation because he was schooling them on the importance of being on point.

Lil Haiti

*"Sleepy, yu stay like a baga Yankee bwoy mek yu*

*parrow,"* said one of the team members, feeling that he

could take on any army of Americans sent his way.

*"Hey, idiot bwoy, wha happen to yu? Dis a foreign*

*whey Yankee, Yardy, Spanish, Haitian, an Bin Laden*

*people dem a one in a thee ghetto,"* said Sleepy, trying to

get his soldier to understand what they were facing.

Explaining that they were on foreign soil and

outnumbered, the members understood that tonight could

be their last day alive, so they said a silent prayer, then

headed for their armored SUVs, only stopping to hear

Sleepy say, *"Nine a we left an nine a we a go backa yard."*

\*\*\*

Positioned behind their rifles in separate locations, both

Young Swiss and Playboy adjusted the sites on their scopes

as they joked over the secure channel on their walkie-talkies, awaiting Divine's signal to let them thangs fly.

Carwin Park was a hot bed for illegal activities, so it was closed by park police at ten o'clock every night, but that meant nothing because the location of the park was in the hood. The fence was there for decoration because it didn't keep anyone out. There were holes cut into it, awarding easy access to enter and leave at will all through the day and night.

Due to the drug trafficking, gambling, and shoot-outs, police presence was heavy on the Haitian, Carwin, and Jamaican sides of Spruce Street, so Divine was risking a trespassing charge and a possession of a firearm way before the drop was intended to take place.

Divine was sitting on a slide, dead smack in the middle of the park, so he could be in sight of Swiss and Playboy. He was itchy to bang and ready to get this whole ordeal over with.

Lil Haiti

At one o'clock in the morning, Divine spotted two black SUVs that he'd never seen before pull up, so he smiled, knowing that it was Ricky's team inside of them, trying to be early to get the possible lay of the land and the drop on who they thought was the kidnapper's partner.

Stepping out of the truck, Sleepy and three others following him walked toward the Trinity building, making sure there weren't any ambushes prepared for them. The other three from the other truck with their weapons drawn headed into the Kentucky Fried Chicken parking lot, unaware of the plain clothes officer, who worked there as a security guard due to the numerous times they were robbed. The last two members of the team headed into the park where they were met by Divine, who pretended not to know who they were when he said, "I have ya money. Now bring me to my wife."

Looking confused, the two gunmen looked at each other, then said, "*A who dis di DJ?*"

"Yeah, I thought you were on the kidnapper's team."

"*No brethren we cum fi Ricky pitny*," said one of the Jamaicans.

The other one said, "*Wha typa fuckery dis? Mi nah understand but mi know mi nah like it.*"

"Look, I got the money right here," said Divine, as he bent down to unzip the duffel bags to show the Jamaicans the money and, at the same time, give Young Swiss and Playboy their green light.

Oblivious to the plain clothes officer calling for back up inside of KFC because of their tremendous amount of fire power, the team of Jamaicans scanned the parking lot, looking for signs of a set up, but none were apparent.

Seeing no signs of life, Sleepy, with his team in tow, doubled back from the Trinity Building, heading toward Carwin Park to see what was good with the drop, but found themselves walking toward a mob of gangstas who came out of Coleman Towers. Looking behind them, Sleepy noticed an even larger mob come out of Trinity, which placed him and his soldiers in a sandwich. They were boxed in until *the* mob behind them crossed the street to position themselves diagonally from their boys to assure that, if a shoot out popped off, there wouldn't be any friendly fire.

Having had the same play in his playbook, Sleepy realized that shit was thick, so he said to who looked like the nigga running shit, "Father, mi nah mean yu no disrespect."

"Yes, you did when you decided to come out here," said the ring leader.

Scared to death, a young boy on Sleepy's team pulled out his weapon while mumbling under his breath, unwillingly creating more tension between the two opposing factions.

"And y'all got guns knowin' that guns mean y'all got bad intentions," said the ring leader, giving his man the signal to get shit poppin'.

The line had been crossed, so before Sleepy could diffuse the situation, both Swiss and Playboy saw Divine's signal and opened fire, slumping the two Jamaicans in the park. Hearing the shots, the angry mobs panicked and opened fire, creating a hail of bullets. There wasn't a thing left to do but fire, so Sleepy and his entourage let their fully automatic weapons ring, dropping a few members of the angry mob.

Shots were exchanged, and lives were taken on both sides, breaking Sleepy's team down to just himself, and at that moment, things got worse because the whole police precinct arrived on Spruce Street, equipped with M16s and M60s ready for war. A three-way shoot out took place with the mob dumping on Sleepy and the police, Sleepy banging on the mob and the police, and the police gunning down anybody black.

Stuck in KFC's parking lot, Swiss-cheesing police cruisers, the three Jamaicans were backed into a corner in the drive through where they held the law at bay for a minute. As their firing pins clicked from empty chambers, doom loomed near, and that was when their lives were taken because the police sent a barrage of .223 shells in their direction, guaranteeing a closed casket. Once the smoke cleared, the police gave one another hi-fives because they were happy to erase three black males from the earth.

Now that the gunfire had ceased, everyone's ears rang because the gunfight was deafening! It sounded like two different fireworks shows from the Fourth of July going off simultaneously.

Sleepy knew he couldn't win, so he fled across the street, but his retreat was cut short when two shots took his life. One shot from Swiss hit him in the neck, and the other from Playboy hit him clear in the heart, killing him before he hit the ground. This was to be his last resting place where he'd lay to be fertilizer for the community garden next to the park. Hearing one of the dying Jamaicans gasp and fight for breath, Divine stood over him, then asked, "Where's Ricky?"

Unaware of Divine's involvement, the Jamaican, in between coughing up blood bubbles, said, *"Him hav a room in a thee Marriot Courtyard."*

Hearing this, Divine ran through a hole in the fence for a short distance until he reached his home girl Kianna's, in the condo complex, next to the park, where he hid for the remainder of the night.

***

"Ring, ring, ring, ring, ring," was all Ricky heard, as he called both Sleepy's and Cashmere's phones.

Frustrated because he couldn't contact anyone, he shouted, "Blood clot!"

Rolling a spliff, then lighting it, he took a deep pull in an attempt to calm his nerves, but his nerves were rocked when he turned on the TV to the Channel Eleven News.

What he saw made the spliff fall from his hand onto his lap as he yelled, "*Ras clot!*"

The reporter informed the citizens that there was a reenactment of World War II on Spruce Street, which had left twelve dead and forty injured.

There was yellow tape everywhere, body bags being carried and, at least, a thousand shell casings behind the reporter, but what stuck out were the two armored SUVs his boys rode in. This scene brought his mind to overdrive, so he now knew the possibilities of what happened out there were endless. Expecting the worst for his squadron, he said a prayer, hoping for their survival, then his mind drifted off to Cashmere and her whereabouts. Her absence was unusual, but before he could pursue figuring it out, his thoughts were broken when he felt his leg burning from the spliff that had fallen on his lap. Shouting *"Bumba!"*, he swatted at the spliff until it hit the ground.

As he was retrieving the spliff, his phone rang, so he ignored the marijuana and rushed to answer in hopes of hearing from either Sleepy or Cashmere, although he felt deep down inside that it wasn't going to be either of them.

Answering the phone, he said, *"A who dis?"*

"If my wife is dead 'cause of ya bullshit, I'm gonna torture you before I kill you," said Divine.

*"DJ, tings gone outta mi control."*

"You think? If you woulda met me like a man, we coulda bounced ideas around until we came up with a conclusion that wouldn't have had such a high body count. You got the streets on fire makin' the police pull over anythin' movin'!"

*"Cool it, DJ. We a get Tessa back. Whey yu dey?"*

"I'm at my stash spot on Mission Street, so come up Mission from Richmond Hill because my spot will be the last house on the right. It's the house before the pay phone behind the Elks Club."

"*Mi hav navigation so mi soon cum.*"

\*\*\*

Hanging up the phone with Divine, the kidnapper said to Tessa, "This whole ordeal is almost over, so be patient. Your husband came through with my money, so you'll be back with your family shortly."

\*\*\*

Arriving at the house Divine described, Ricky hopped out, looked around, and thought something was wrong because the house looked abandoned. The looks of the house made him hear the words of his old friend and spiritual advisor Smitty when he would say, *"Di bwoy di devil!"* The words echoed through his head for a while but subsided when a porch light flickered on and off as an indication that there was life inside the house.

Seeing this, Ricky proceeded with caution around the side of the house to the back door with his gun drawn, but during his walk, he spotted two pitbulls through a basement window pacing back and forth. This visual only enhanced his feelings of unease. Finally climbing up the back stairs onto the porch where Divine waited with a Guinness in his hand, he said, *"DJ, wha typa fuckery dis?"*

"Relax, old man, 'cause everythin' ain't what it seems. This is my lap of luxury," said Divine, as he gestured for Ricky to enter, and when he did, shock was written all over his face because the interior and the exterior of the house didn't match one another.

The house's interior was equipped with a five-star kitchen stocked with a Viking range, Whirlpool appliances, Kitchen Aid pots and pans, and an extravagant living room laced with high-end Italian leather sofas. Sony flat screens and a state-of-the-art surround sound system put the icing on the cake, so Ricky said, *"Dis yah nice, my yout."*

Taking a seat at the solid cherry wood dining room table, they sipped Guinness and Hennessy Paradis as Divine voiced how he didn't like Ricky's approach to getting Tessa back. His approach had gotten a bunch of innocent people killed or injured. Listening closely and soaking in every word, Ricky said, *"Mi understand, DJ. Di road pon fiya! Mi see x-amounta Babylon an dem hav check point on every corner."*

"My people are closer than close to findin' where he's keepin' her, so we'll be knee deep in his ass soon."

*"Hmm. Yu tink she all right?"* asked Ricky, with his voice cracking from fear at the thought of losing his baby.

"She better be 'cause, if she's ain't, I'll keep my promise of killin' you."

"*Cool it, DJ. Mi wan her back jus like yu wan her back.*"

"I hope so."

"*Stop yu foolish talk, my yout. Everyting crisp.*"

"A'ight. I'm getting some more Henny, you straight?" said Divine, heading to the bar behind where Ricky was seated.

"*Yeah, mon,*" he said, without turning his attention to Divine.

Seeing his opportunity to subdue Ricky, he grabbed the baseball bat that was placed behind the bar for drunk guests who got out of control. Gripping the bat tightly, he eased over to Ricky and swung hard enough to hit a ball over the green monster at Fenway, knocking Ricky unconscious.

After laying Ricky out, he dragged him down to the basement where he tied him to a cement pillar that was conveniently located only six inches away from the maximum reach of two pit bulls' leashes. The purpose for this was to scare Ricky close to a heart attack when he awoke to see the dogs charging toward him with their razor-sharp fangs exposed.

He remained unconscious for fifteen minutes before Divine threw a bucket of ice water on him, which awoke every nerve in his body. While unconscious, he'd dreamt of Smitty and all of his warnings, so when he awoke from his slumber, he groggily asked, "*Wha gwon, DJ?*"

"You don't remember, do you?"

"*Member wha?*"

"You don't recognize my face, do you? Well, I'll remind you. Twenty-six years ago, you ran up in a bodega with one of ya cronies and killed my father. Does that ring a bell?"

367

*"DJ, yu gone mad from Hennessy."*

"Oh, really, don't you remember this?" he asked, pointing to the lion head medallion on his chain. "When I was four years old, holdin' my dyin' father in my arms, you shot and killed your partner-in-crime, then fled only doublin' back because this chain that was hangin' from my father's neck caught your eye. Luckily the police cruisers were close, forcin' you to flee. This chain was my father's, and that's why it looked so familiar to you when you saw it in Jamaica."

*"Bumba clot! Now mi understand. Dis a small world when yu kill a mon an him pitny breed up yu pitny,"* said Ricky, shaking his head in disbelief.

"I knew you'd remember after a short trip down memory lane. Now that you remember, it's time for me to feed my dogs 'cause they haven't eaten in a while," he said, as he snapped his fingers to alert the dogs.

Seeing what Divine had in mind, he began to squirm in an attempt to set himself free, but it didn't work, because Divine had earned merit badges for displaying proficiency at tying knots back when he was a boy scout.

Watching Ricky's feeble attempt at escaping made him laugh. Then, he said to the dogs, "Watch him!"

Foaming at their mouths, the dogs barked and growled, displaying teeth so sharp they looked as if they were filed to a point. This horrific scene was too much for Ricky to stomach, so he said, "*DJ, yu nah affi do it like dis.*"

His pleading fell on uninterested ears because Divine said, "Did I ask you to talk? You a bitch-ass nigga! My pops didn't cop pleas, so take it like a man! Fuck this shit! Gemini! Homicide! Eat!"

Obeying their commands, they darted toward him, and he screamed like a bitch. He hit octaves no other Jamaican in the whole existence of the world had hit.

Gemini leaped for his neck, so Ricky closed his eyes as a feeling of defeat enveloped him. Homicide, on the other hand, lunged for one of his arms seeming to think it was an appetizer. The thought of being torn to shreds was crippling but hearing Divine's laughter in between the barking of the dogs awarded him a brief reprieve. Surprised to be in one piece, he noticed that the dogs were extremely close, but weren't close enough to devour him, so he took in a deep breath as a sigh of relief.

"Do you think I would make it that easy for you?" asked Divine as he scratched Gemini behind the ear.

"*Fuck yu, Haitian bwoy!*"

"You sound like a bitch when you scream, and I don't like the tone of ya voice right now. I sense a lot of hostility when you speak, so I think it's time to shut you up," he said, as he gagged Ricky's mouth.

Slowly walking over to a pair of shears, he examined them, then headed back to his victim, who wore a lot of gold rings, then snipped off two fingers. Picking up

the fingers, he removed the rings, then threw a finger to

each of the dogs, and they gobbled them up greedily.

Big beads of sweat dripped from Ricky's brow as

the excruciating pain surged through his body. The pain

was unbearable, so he squirmed in place as if he had to use

the bathroom while Divine said, "My dogs are big, so I'm

not gonna be here throwin' them treats when that will only

piss them off. They don't like to be pissed, so enough with

the games. I gave them their appetizer, so get ready to give

up their entrée."

Watching his assailant pick up an axe, his eyes grew

to the size of golf balls, shook by what this crazy Haitian

had in store. Handling the axe like a seasoned lumber jack,

Divine said,

"I never done this before, but I think that, as long as I keep

choppin' fire wood in my mind's eye, this shouldn't be too

difficult."

Witnessing Divine raise the axe over his shoulder was one thing, but Ricky pissed on himself when he saw the blade coming down in his direction. The axe was so sharp he didn't feel a thing when it pierced through his flesh and bone, so he believed this was another scare tactic used to rattle his nerves. What made him reconsider that notion was the same thing that made him pass out. Seeing his kneecap get picked up then tossed to the dogs as they fought for it was enough to make his lights go out, and that was exactly what happened.

Leaving him unconscious, Divine went upstairs to the shed where he retrieved an extension cord, circular skill saw, and apron to keep clean while carving himself a yardy. Taking his time as he went back down to the basement, Divine thought about his father, and this quickly motivated him to get the job done. Back in the basement, he slapped life into Ricky. Then he said, "Ya a very rude guest. How dare you fall asleep at the dinin' room table? Don't sweat it, though 'cause I woke you up in time for the main course.

Do you know what our guests Gemini and Homicide love?

I doubt you do, so I'll tell you. They love ribs, so ribs it is."

Squeezing and holding the trigger to the circular saw to allow it maximum speed, Divine had a maniacal look on his face, and it scared Ricky more than what was to happen next. He saw the devil or something more evil in Divine's eyes, so he knew his life was over. Shortly after the thought vanished from his mind, he felt the blade tear through his skin, then his bones, as Divine cut out perfect squares of his ribs, ensuring the dogs received equal shares.

Limp and lifeless, Ricky hung from the pillar, dead, so Divine untied him, then removed the dogs' leashes to give them free reign of the basement, so they could snack on him as they pleased.

Freshening up after his butchering was completed, Divine left the evil spirits behind, burned the bloody clothes, and headed upstate to Armonk, New York, in order to rescue his baby.

\*\*\*

After giving Divine directions to the cottage, the kidnapper hung up the phone and said, "Mrs. Jean-Baptiste, your nightmare will be over in about forty-five minutes so be patient. I'm sorry we had to meet like this, but I must be going."

Leaving her tied to a chair, the kidnapper slid out the back door, leaving her alone for what she thought would be an eternity.

\*\*\*

Flying up 287, Divine cut the ride down to a half-hour because he was anxious to see his lovely Tessa. Reaching the cottage, he jumped out, leaving the car door opened with his gun drawn, ready to save his baby. After kicking in the door, he saw his beautiful Tessa frightened but okay, tied to a chair, so he rushed to her side assuring her that she was safe. Once she was freed from her restraints, she gave him the biggest hug, then said, "Baby, I'm so sorry I walked out on us before I gave you a chance to explain. Oh, baby, I have so much to say. Let's renew our vows ... let's ..."

Cutting her off by placing a finger over her lips, he said, "Shhh! Relax. I'm here, and I know how deep our love is, so you don't have any reason to explain. Now with that being said, let's get outta here."

Carrying his lovely lady to his BMW M6, he gently placed her on the soft leather seat of his passenger side, then took off in the direction of his mother's house to reunite Tessa with their little girls.

# Chapter 8

# Two Weeks Later

"Dearly beloved, we are gathered here today, not to mourn, but to celebrate the life of Ricardo Thomas. He was a great friend, father, and grandfather. This man touched a world of people in a special way. He had a contagious laugh and a personality that made everyone smile and enjoy his company. He provided for his daughter and grandchildren like no other, so he was deeply appreciated. Let's bow our heads in a moment of silence, shall we?" said Reverend Davis.

Bowing his head while comforting Tessa, Divine thought the sermon was a crock of shit because Ricky had touched a lot of people but in the wrong way. The bastard had killed his father, so he didn't feel the lies that were being preached. You can say he was remorseless because he knew in advance that his wife's heart would be hurting on this day, but his retribution was to come first, and he'd deal with her sorrow when that bridge came to pass. He knew her pain firsthand because he'd been through it, but he still did what was necessary to mend the heart that was broken twenty-six years ago.

Across from where Divine was located with Tessa and the kids, Detective McNeil watched him with a curious eye. Speaking to his partner, he said, "I don't trust him. He seems too cool about this situation while it's clear that his wife is suffering. I have a hunch that he's our guy. What confirms this hunch is the fact that we've received information that Ricardo was the number one suspect in the slaying of young Divine's father. That homicide has been a closed case for twenty-six years, and it will remain closed, but I refuse to let Mr. Jean-Baptiste get away with Ricardo's murder! Too many bodies have dropped recently, and there will be hell to pay if I don't get any answers.

There's no way I'm letting this madness happen under my watch without repercussions."

Breaking down, Tessa wailed like a banshee screaming, "Dad, no! Why is this happening? I want to go with you!"

Grabbing her at the right moment to prevent her from jumping onto the casket, Divine escorted her and the girls to their limo and exited the cemetery, unaware of the hound dog sniffing his trail.

"I'm going to nail your Haitian ass to the cross under the jail, Divine. You're an animal if you can put your wife and daughters through this type of turmoil," said Detective McNeil.

# Chapter 9

# Six Months Later

"This cookout poppin'!" said Swiss, as he sipped on a Guinness.

"Hell, yeah! Tessa's steaks be slammin' and S-Alive's people brought them bangin' ass ribs where the meat falls off the bone!" said Playboy.

"Yes! It is I, the magnificent!" said T-Gunz, baring gifts for all the kids at the cookout.

In unison, Playboy and Swiss said, "Damn, nigga! Where you been at?" as they ran over to give him pounds and hugs.

"I'm around, so don't think, 'cause you don't see me, I'm out the loop," he said, knowing they'd read in between the lines and understood what he was saying.

"Gunz, what up?" asked Divine, sounding like a sample of Sheek Louch.

"I'm good. How you?"

"I'm good, homie. Walk with me 'cause I need to scream at you," said Divine, as he put his arm around Gunz's shoulder.

Stepping off to outside of ear's range, Divine said, "Good lookin' for doin' that snatch and grab."

"It was nothin', B. You woulda done the same for me. But on some other shit, how she doin'? She ain't traumatized, is she? I tried my best to keep her calm. I even cooked Haitian food for her. You should've seen her fuckin' that shit up!"

"Nah, she straight. What you mean you cooked for her, nigga? You tryin' to take my bitch? I know how ya cookin' taste, so you shoulda let her starve. She fuck around be dreaming about that good shit," he said jokingly. Sharing a laugh while sipping their Guinness, Divine asked,

"How you know somebody was gonna be in the fifth floor staircase?"

"That nigga stay in the staircase. Ray-Ro owed me $4,500 for a duffel bag of bangas I gave him on the strength of him having beef with the whole town. I was tired of his ducking me, so it is what it is. That nigga live in the staircase, but whenever I came to collect, somebody would hit him on the chirp, and he'd be gone by the time I got to the fifth floor."

"It is what it is, but what about son at Southfield?"

"You can't be serious, Divine! Did you watch the news?"

"Yeah, so what?"

"Didn't you recognize the name?"

"Nah, who that?"

"That's the little nigga that ran out ya whip back in the day, gettin' you those four calendars."

"Oh, shit!! I ain't seen that nigga since then."

"I told you, 'I got you, my nigga.' You didn't really think I was lettin' that go down, did you?"

"I love you, my nigga!"

"I know. On some other shit, though, I'm tired. I'm tired of the streets. You still got room for me in this music shit? If so, I'm ready to get this music money."

"Took ya ass long enough," said Divine, as they went back to join the rest of the people who were enjoying themselves.

\*\*\*

Two weeks after the cookout, things seemed to be back to normal, but Tessa dropped a bombshell on her husband when she said, "Divine, we need to talk."

"Scream at me, love," he said, as he gave her a big hug.

"Boy, this is serious."

"I know, and that's why I'm squeezin' this big ole booty. This big ole thang is the cushion that's gonna brace me from the impact of what ya 'bout to say."

"That's what I hate about you, Divine. I'm not joking. This is serious business."

"I'm sorry, bae. What's wrong?"

"How well do you know that guy who brought gifts for all the kids at the cookout the other day?"

"Who Gunz? That's my brother, why?"

"That's him, Divine. That's who kidnapped me!"

"What!? Tessa, ya buggin'! That's my family! That's like sayin' Playboy kidnapped you."

"I know that voice and those eyes, Divine! I'm a thousand percent sure! Baby, you have to believe me and trust my instincts," said Tessa, as she squeezed him tight for comfort.

Knowing that she was right, he quickly said, "I'll look into it, and if it was him, his life will come to an end."

Standing there with her head in his chest sharing a warm embrace with the love of his life, Divine's mind raced like the vehicles at the Indy 500. And since her head was in his chest, she couldn't see the worry plastered across his face, and that was a plus for him because, if she had looked up to see his expression, she'd have killed him with her bare hands. The expression on his face showed that it was evident he was involved in all the wrongdoing going on around her.

Sensing their embrace was about to end, he quickly put on his game face before she looked into his eyes to say, "Baby, I want retribution!"

Lil Haiti

Made in the USA
Middletown, DE
02 April 2021

36762574R00216